I0663322

THE DEFINING SEA

BOOK 2 OF THE PUERTO RICO TRILOGY

ROBERT FRIEDMAN

BROWN POSEY PRESS

an imprint of Sunbury Press, Inc.
Mechanicsburg, PA USA

an imprint of Sunbury Press, Inc.
Mechanicsburg, PA USA

For information about special discounts for bulk purchases, please contact Sunbury Press Orders Dept. at (855) 338-8359 or orders@sunburypress.com.

To request one of our authors for speaking engagements or book signings, please contact Sunbury Press Publicity Dept. at publicity@sunburypress.com.

ISBN: 978-1-62006-008-7 (Trade paperback)

Library of Congress Control Number: 2019936509

FIRST BROWN POSEY PRESS EDITION: February 2019

Product of the United States of America
0 1 1 2 3 5 8 13 21 34 55

Set in Bookman Old Style
Designed by Crystal Devine
Cover by Terry Kennedy
Edited by Lawrence Knorr

Continue the Enlightenment!

PART ONE

ONE

What began political turned deathly personal.

It started off disciplined, full of energy, even inspiring, before it blew all to pieces.

We were protesting the Navy bombing the hell out of Vieques, the small, inhabited island that belongs to Puerto Rico. The maneuvers had killed a resident and were poisoning the water, the land, and the air. Fishermen couldn't fish. People were suffering from breathing and heart diseases. Kids were getting cancer.

The pro-independence students had started the rally by the west gate, with the usual speeches against U.S. imperialism. Then we marched down the main pathway between the majestic palms to the University clock tower, which rose over the large campus, spread through the San Juan suburb of Río Piedras. We mounted the steps to the tower and went through the portico and down the hallway and started chanting, "Navy, Go Home," as though there were a bunch of admirals in the offices located in the tower's first two floors instead of the university's bureaucrats. We exited on the portico's left side and moved across the campus, picking up lots more protestors along the way.

Leading the march and waving a huge Puerto Rican flag was Pito Gómez, head of the University's pro-independence student organization. As he shouted for the island's freedom, a vein bolted from under his black beret down the center of his forehead. I even spotted some pro-statehood students among the demonstrators. We were well over a hundred, marching through the quad toward the University Theater, raising fists, chanting "U. S., Out of Vieques," blowing whistles, scraping *guiros*, slapping hand drums and sweating just a little. The sun was pleasantly simmering in a bright blue, cloudless sky.

Party time—sort-of.

I left the marchers to get Laura after her class in *Latin American Literature, the Boom* (García Márquez, Donoso, Cabrera Infante, Cortázar, etc.). She stood by the bulletin board outside the Humanities Building in the quad, so lovely in her yellow blouse tucked into dark jeans, her soft brown hair tied with a green ribbon in the back. Sort of short, sort of thin, except where she shouldn't be. Holding a couple of novels under her arm. She gave me a big hug. The demonstration was really taking off, I told her. Not only the extreme lefties, but *everyone* was joining in.

The truth was that Laura wasn't all that keen on demonstrating. "These people are always doing the wrong things for the right reasons," she said.

The demonstration last week had ended with the "invasion" of classes and the shouting down of the professors. I couldn't disagree. But the cause, I said, was growing. The means weren't so pretty, but in this case, the end was more than justified. We had to show solidarity.

She nodded gravely. Those large green-gray eyes in that small, soulful face looked at me, as though weighing not only what I had just said, but everything about me. Then she surrendered a sweet smile. "Solidarity," she said.

She knew how to invade and occupy my heart.

When we met up with the others, the good vibes were fast evaporating. The festive air was turning toxic. The University guards surrounded the quad, trying to hem us in so we couldn't break out again to other parts of the campus. A beefy guard viciously slammed his baton against the legs of a chanting female student who the guard thought was getting too close to him. She grabbed an ankle and hopped around, then collapsed in the center of the quad. Tears ran down her cheeks. Insults were hurled at the guard—"¡cabrón!" "¡hijo de la gran puta!"—while the other guards looked on stone-faced behind large sunglasses, nervously tapping their batons against their palms and their thighs. Laura tightened her grip on my hand.

Then the guards got orders on their walkie-talkies and started backing off. They climbed into their vehicles on the road behind the theater and took off. We cheered but wondered why the withdrawal. We soon found out.

A few minutes later, the Riot Squad invaded the campus. They rolled up in vans and armored cars on the road just behind the theater and jumped from the vehicles. They wore visored dark helmets and plastic face shields. Bulletproof vests covered their short-sleeved blue shirts. They carried long see-through body shields and clubs and shotguns.

The chicken-shit administration had called in the Darth Vader stormtroopers, an over-reaction, to say the least. That was too much for most of us. When a rock smashed through the front window of a van parked just outside the quad, I cheered with the rest of the protestors.

Laura wasn't cheering. Her smile was shaky. It was, I believe, a disappointed smile; disappointed, I guess, that I could so easily lose my usual cool to become part of the jeering, cheering crowd. I felt sort of guilty.

But the cops weren't stressing out over feelings. While rocks and bottles banged off their shields and helmets, they waded into us, swinging their clubs, bringing students down with blows to the front and the back of the knees, bloodying heads. A tall, thin guy with his glasses hanging from one bloodied ear stumbled around the quad, falling against the busts of the three poets on pedestals there. He was swatting the air in front of him like he was trying to get rid of a swarm of mosquitoes. A cop grabbed the swinging arm and twisted it back until something cracked and another cop had his arm across a girl's chest, pulling her back against him. When she tumbled at his feet, he grabbed her hair and dragged her across the grass.

Then came the popping from the tear-gas canisters. Laura and I panicked like the others and, hand-in-sweaty-hand, we tried to break out of the quad. Our faces dampened with tears and snot. We were coughing like we were choking. Then the cop's club slammed across my shoulders and I let go of Laura's hand; I flew forward, staggering along while trying to stay on my feet.

I collapsed on my knees. When I turned to look for Laura, I saw a fat bastard put his club around her neck and pull her backward. Her hands went up like she was saying she surrendered. The motherfucking cop was three times Laura's size. Her eyes looked like they were going to pop out of her head.

I lost my breath, then got it back, and pulled myself up—for about two seconds. A cop in a plastic mask bent over and began smashing my body with a club. I tried to cover my face with my arms and the club came down on my head. The club went up again and then a hand grabbed it and I heard: "That's enough!"

I have no idea how Professor Camacho got there, but there he was, wrestling with the cop. The cop pulled the club free and raised it again, about to smash it down on the prof, but something made him hesitate and instead, he turned and chased down another student, clubbing him across the back.

The prof helped me to my feet and pulled me under the portico of the Home Economics Building across from Humanities. I watched students walking around the quad dazed and moaning. I couldn't see Laura anywhere.

A Molotov cocktail was tossed into a police van and exploded the van into flame.

Then a gunshot; then another, and another.

I'm not sure where the first shot came from, but the cops started shooting at a building in the quad. Another Molotov cocktail exploded in one of the Riot Squad vans. The cops started shooting into the crowd. I limped back into the quad, looking for Laura, searching the prone and the sitting figures, some with their heads in their hands, others with their heads lolling back on their necks. It looked like a battlefield with the wounded lying all over. People were screaming at those still in the quad to get shelter from the gunfire. Some crawled away to the porticos of the buildings.

I stayed in the quad, crouched and running from one side to the other.

I couldn't find Laura.

Then I limped around from building to building: searching the crowded porticos. I couldn't find her. My heart was jumping in my chest. Where the hell did she go?

She was on the concrete path between the Humanities building and the University Theater. One arm was twisted beneath her body and one leg was half-bent and touching the other. She looked like a life-sized, broken doll. Blood and some other stuff covered her left cheek and the shoulder of her blouse. It ran through the soft down on her arm. I thought, stupidly, if I kissed her I could bring her back to life. I bent my head toward her lips. They were still warm and moist. She must still be . . . I looked around, shouted, bent toward her again, kissed her, yelled at the top of my lungs.

"A student was accidentally shot and killed and a policeman was wounded by shrapnel from an exploding vehicle after the Riot

Squad was called onto the campus to quell a demonstration that turned violent, threatening life and property."

That was the fuckin University's press release.

When Laura's life ended, my world contracted into this incredibly tight ball. At first, it wasn't pain so much as a heavy numbness. When I woke each morning, I was sure it hadn't happened. Still, I didn't want the day to continue because I knew that I would, of course, realize what did happen and it would start again, crawling and scraping around inside me and dragging me to the edge of that hollow space, so painful because it sucked in everything and yet was so vacant.

My fault. Mea fuckin culpa.

It's been one year. I'm still working toward making sure that people remember what happened on that day, May 22, 1999. That they remember the martyred, the loving Laura Rosario.

I'd make damn sure they remembered.

TWO

At one minute to the start of his class, Ralph Camacho pulled his 15-year-old Corolla into a faculty space near the University Tower. A nice breeze was ruffling the fronds of the royal palms. The cicadas were chirping and the tree frogs coqui-ing in the soft evening air as he rushed off to the Humanities Building.

He didn't bother calling the roll. Two of the fifteen students who took the course were absent. Richie Pérez hadn't shown up now for the last four classes. Strange, considering that Richie hadn't previously missed Ralph's class in the last two semesters. He'd shown up even after that terrible day.

They were tracing the Puerto Rican Diaspora through great tales of the sea, exploring how the quests related to primal and universal desires and—why not?—to their own lives. They were currently sailing over the pages of *The Argonautica,* accompanying Jason in pursuit of the Golden Fleece.

When the bell rang, the students took off and Ralph gathered up the papers on his desk. When he looked up, he saw a woman in dark slacks, a bright red blouse and red shoes standing in the back of the room. She was a big woman, tall and ample-bodied, maybe in her mid-forties, her auburn hair piled on top her head. She looked vaguely familiar.

"Can I help you?"

The woman walked up to the desk. "May I talk to you?"

"Of course."

She looked nervous.

"We met a year ago," the woman said. "At the funeral of the girl, the one who . . ."

Richie's mother! "You're Señora Pérez."

The woman nodded. "My son speaks very highly of you. Both as a professor and, he says, as 'a humane human'."

Ralph shrugged, as though no great effort went into his "humanity." Then, feeling he was minimizing Richie's honest sentiment, he smiled widely. "That's very nice," he said.

"He deeply respects you."

The woman's lips were painted almost as red as her blouse and her large dark brown eyes were heavy with mascara. Her full cheeks looked powdered. Ralph felt a little sad that she felt she had to use so much makeup for the meeting.

"Is Richie O.K.?"

"That's what I've come to see you about," said Richie's mother. "I haven't been able to get in touch with him for several days."

"He hasn't been in class recently."

"Have you heard from him?" she asked hopefully. "Do you know where he might have gone?"

"No. He hasn't contacted me."

Señora Pérez took a deep breath. "You know, Richie shares an apartment with a friend not too far from the campus. I live out in Arecibo, where I work at the City Hall as a receptionist. We talk every day. But all this week he hasn't answered his cell phone. I took off work today. His friend told me Richie hasn't been at the apartment for two weeks! He said Richie told him he was going on a trip but would be back soon. His friend said Richie didn't say where he was going. But we spoke every day two weeks ago and Richie said nothing about going anywhere. He called last Saturday. He said nothing unusual. He even said he would try to come to see me in the next few weekends. He hasn't called since. I keep getting the voicemail on his cell phone. I'm really worried. I don't know what to do. Should I go to the police? I don't know!"

The tears came from the corners of her eyes. Her cheeks began to streak with the dark mascara. "He's never done this before. I don't know where to turn."

Ralph looked out the window. The purple sky already was turning black. The first stars were shining through. "I don't know if the police will be able to do anything," he said.

"So what do I do? Can you help me?" In the woman's pleading eyes, besides the beseeching look, there was something tenacious, almost demanding.

"Will you help find my son?"

"I'll try."

What else could he say?

THREE

The flight was going smooth. The turbulence was in my stomach. An acidy stomach could cause the latex to disintegrate, the capsules could leak, burst—that would be it.

I had the burning inside, bile floating around in my chest and sliding up into my throat, rotten eggs and metal in my mouth. I could feel the heavy stuff moving around inside and I wanted to puke it out.

I stumbled down the aisle to the back of the plane and into a bathroom. I gagged over the toilet bowl. Nothing came up. I tried again. Burning scraped around my chest and throat, but only a little spittle came up. My heart was galloping. I scrunched my head under the faucet of the tiny sink. I dried my face and neck with paper towels, staggered back to my seat.

I told myself it was just nerves. Calm down.

I've mostly transported it in luggage—you check the bag at the airline counter in San Juan like any other passenger and the baggage handlers receiving payoffs take care of it getting on the plane. Then, just like the other passengers, you pick it up in New York at the luggage carousel. When you land in the states from Puerto Rico there's no customs to go through. You just take your bag to the nearest exit, smiling all the way at the other passengers and the guards at the door, just another Puerto Rican kid happy to be coming back to El Barrio for a visit. Then you make the drop where you're supposed to. For me, it was that same hotel on the Upper West Side.

A couple of times it got more complicated. Like this last time, when I had to first fly to the D.R. because of a shortage in Puerto Rico—the feds had seized several coke-loaded *yolas* in the Mona

Passage. So I swallowed the drugs in Santo Domingo, then got on the plane to New York.

Swallowing drugs isn't easy. But, like anything else, you learn. The drugs are wrapped in condoms, tied off with dental floss. You dip the pellets in salad oil and if you stay calm, you can get them down without gagging too much. The first time was hell; it took me hours. This time they sprayed my throat to numb the gullet and I got used to feeling the weight.

Before getting on the plane, I took some Lomotil, so I wouldn't shit it all out before I got to New York. Like always, I didn't eat on the plane, just drank some water and plugged in the earphones. But this time, I was really nervous, probably because this would be my last trip. Just this trip and I'd have over $20,000. That would be it. Definitely! I'd be out, clear and clean.

But an acidy stomach can really ruin you. I'd probably die before the friggin' plane landed!

So now I was breathing deeply, telling myself it was mind over whatever was fucking up my insides. Before the flight, I even took antacid medicine.

We were beginning our descent and the plane shook from side to side and my stomach was twisting and turning until, finally, we broke through the clouds and rattled and braked to a landing.

I survived. My stomach was now calm as a summer lake, *gracias a Dios*.

I took a taxi to the hotel. Before going up to the room, I went to a drug store and bought the chocolate type laxative. The last time the laxative wasn't working too well and I had to take an enema. I hoped like hell this wouldn't happen again.

When I got to the hotel room, the same two guys from the other trips were there, waiting. They greeted me with a couple of grunts. It was about nine p.m. and I was pooped and told them I wanted to go to bed, so I would be O.K. in the morning when I started delivering the drugs. A cot had been set up between the two beds in the room and I was told to sack out on it. My stomach started churning slightly, but I fell asleep, in my clothes, almost immediately.

At about six the next morning I started crapping the coke-filled capsules. I did it in the bathtub so that none of the capsules would slip down the toilet bowl. By eleven, I finished shitting them all out, washing them with toothpaste, scrubbing down the tub and counting the capsules. Ninety came out, which was the amount of capsules I swallowed in Santo Domingo. I told that to the guys as I was gathering up the capsules and putting them into Ziploc bags.

"Sorry, m'ijo," said Junior, a big fleshy guy with tiny eyes. "We waitin' on one hundred coming from out your ass or other places. You don't deliver in full, we got to hold you here until we get word to Papo."

"Hey, I swallowed the ninety I got in the D.R.," I said. "That's what they gave me. Check it out with Manny El Bronx, who set up the trip and everything. I counted every one going down and every friggin' one's here."

"The information we have is that you swallowed a hundred," said Junior.

"That's bullshit!" My pellet-less bowels were starting to stir again.

"Now he's fuckin with us," said the other guy, Chucho, who looked just a couple of years older than me. "Now we got to wait for Papo. Goddamn!" He kept making snorting sounds.

"We were told you took down one hundred," Junior said. "You fuck with us, it ain't gonna be pretty for you, I guarantee."

I put out my hands, palms up. "I swear . . ."

"Yeah, they all do," Junior gave me a sad look.

Chucho, who was six inches short of my five-foot-ten and about forty pounds lighter, looked like he was ready to tear into me. He moved from one leg to the other and rubbed his hands together, like he was anticipating—something. He went into his pants pocket and brought out a long switchblade and clicked it open. "Let's cut him open to see if the others are still in there," he said.

Junior, holding his cell phone to his ear, ignored Chucho, who gave me a dirty look and clicked the knife closed.

We spent the next hour waiting. I lay on the bed, my arms behind my head. Junior and Chucho were watching Jerry Springer and the freak parade on TV. Some guy dressed as a woman said two weeks ago he pretended he was a hooker so he could "have relations" with his older brother who he was in love with. His older brother, a short, stocky guy, shot up from his chair, knocking it over, and lunged at his tall and skinny cross-dressing younger brother. Springer's musclemen had to pull him off. I was trying to look bored. But my stomach kept twisting and turning and I got up to go to the bathroom two or three more times.

"You shit out the missing ones?" Junior kept asking.

"I *told* you, man . . ."

There had to be a misunderstanding on the drug delivery. There had been no problem on the other trips. Maybe if I called Manny . . . But I didn't have his phone number. I figured those guys must have it.

"Why don't you call . . .?"

"Why don't you shut the fuck up," Chucho said. "We're waitin' to hear from Papo."

After a couple more minutes, the room phone rang. Junior picked it up, listened, said, "Yeah" a few times, then hung up. "He's downstairs. Let's go."

When we got downstairs, a balding, middle-aged guy with a big chest and a hairpin mustache waited at the elevator door. Although it was a nice spring day, he was wearing a long leather jacket. His eyes were covered by aviator's sunglasses.

"I took care of the hotel bill," he said. "Let's go, I still got lots of shit to do. And I'm in a no-parking zone."

We stepped out of the hotel. The car, a dark green Mercedes, was parked right on Broadway. A policewoman with a big behind was writing up a ticket.

"*Fuck!*" said Papo, who as a dealer in the Big Apple and parts of Jersey could probably have afforded several parking tickets a day. He told Chucho and Junior to take my arms like they were holding me up from passing out and to wait on the sidewalk. Chucho pulled his switchblade out of his pocket and, while holding my arm with one hand, tipped the open blade against my back. Papo went up to the policewoman with outstretched arms. His head moved back and forth like he was a Jewish man praying.

The policewoman frowned and shook her head. Papo kept talking, shaking his head also. The policewoman looked over to us. Papo pointed to me. His smile disappeared and his face drooped in sadness. He took a handkerchief out of his jacket's side pocket and blew his nose. The policewoman stopped writing. Papo jerked his head for us to move to the car.

We got in the back seat, me in the middle. Papo got behind the wheel. "We're taking the kid directly to the hospital, to detox," he said. "I don't know what I'm going to tell Mom. Officer, you're an angel. I'd like to show my appreciation." He dug into his pants pocket and pulled out a thick wallet.

The policewoman put up a hand like she was stopping traffic. "Just get the hell out of here."

"Thanks, officer," said Papo, zipping the Mercedes out into traffic.

"Why the hell can't they all be like that?" he asked, shaking his head, angry that they weren't.

Papo was alone up front and the three of us were squeezed in the back. We headed down Broadway, through Times Square, then down to the Avenue of the Americas and through the Village. Papo was cursing the slow-moving traffic. We turned on Canal Street, crept forward, moved through the Holland Tunnel, then got onto the Turnpike. We were heading towards Jersey. Great! They probably would dump me off the side of the road. Would I be shot or knifed? I fought back the tears.

"Let me tell you what the deal is," Papo said, staring straight ahead. "First, I want you to know, I'm a very busy man, and you are putting me out *tremendously.* You're lucky that I got some business I could take care of where we're going, or you would have been dumped in a ditch off the Turnpike. But I believe in giving a young guy like you a second chance because we were all young guys on the make once, and I got a kid your age, *tu sabes*? So I'm goin' out of my way here, and we're taking you to a house, where, if we have to, we could do whatever we want with you without nobody inquiring. What you done here is a serious offense. Ten capsules, about ten grams a capsule, street value of $10,000 for the ten. Which means, of course, you don't get the $5,000 for the trip. Plus all the heartache you put everyone through means you owe us $10,000 for the *perico* and, let's say, another $5,000 for the heartache. Which means you are into me for $15,000. Which, if you don't come up with, then, well, I think you get the idea. I got the *Colombianos* on my ass for payment on what you brought up and I always keep my books balanced and never—and I mean *never*—let a punk mule fuck me out of one cent! *Entiendes?*"

"I gave you all that was given to me," I said. "I swallowed ninety and you got ninety capsules. You can call . . ."

"Shut the fuck up and think how you're going to come up with the ten capsules or the $15,000," Papo ordered.

How the fuck was I going to come up with either? I had to squeeze back what was loosening in my bowels, as though my insides wanted to show Papo they were fully cooperating, no capsules were left in there.

I didn't say anything. We got off the Turnpike, went through a few towns and past never-ending shopping centers, then finally got onto a road that led through the Pine Barrens. The thick forest area covers almost a quarter of New Jersey, the most crowded state on the U.S. mainland. I learned that in school when we lived in Bayonne for a year after we left the Bronx, where we returned the next year.

We moved to Jersey because Mom got what she thought was a better job in the front office of a shipping company. In truth, she took the job because the guy who ran the company, Murray Feinstein, was dating her. That pissed me off. I guess I was jealous. She was showing someone else loving attention besides me. Anyway, they broke up and we moved back to the Bronx. I'm one more PR who got his upbringing in New York, in the Bronx. Stickball, hockey on roller skates, Orchid Beach with my skinny body in the summer, making out in the hallways, delivering groceries for Don Felipe, smoking pot on the roofs, seeing friends fuck up their own and other lives with the stronger stuff (like Jimmy Sanabria, who played great trumpet, even sat in one night with Tito Puente, and popped pills, sniffed coke, then went to mainlining heroin and one drugged-up night drove himself, his girlfriend Zaida and the baby in her stomach off the Willis Avenue bridge). Lucky for me, I was getting high on playing baseball while opening a school book only the night before tests. My mind only opened up, at least as far as reading books and getting politically involved, when we returned to Puerto Rico. Mom's cousin helped her get a job there and I started at the University. My emotions, the real, deepest, most tender ones, opened when I met Laura.

Those eyes looking into mine, as though she were willing to share with me whatever she felt at the moment.

We came to the town of Toms River in South Jersey. I was still scared shitless, but I was starting to feel numb too. What'll happen,'ll happen. Fuck it.

We went down a highway bordered by the usual strip malls and Wawa food markets and took a road out of Toms River. We were heading to the shore. We pulled up in front of a nice-looking, white-painted, two-story house with steps leading up to the second floor. Down the block was a boardwalk and, beyond that, the glistening ocean.

"This is a vacation home," said Papo. "Your vacation is going to consist of you being chained to the bed upstairs."

No one was laughing.

I wasn't chained, but I was locked in the upstairs bedroom. After having patted me down and going through my shoulder bag when we'd left the hotel room, this time they searched me more closely. I'd brought a change of clothes, like I always do on these trips, even though I return the evening of the same day, or early the next morning. I also had a copy of the book I was reading, *The Wretched of the Earth*. They let me keep the clothes and the book and took my cell phone, my return ticket to Puerto Rico and my American Express credit card. Since I got paid in cash for the other drug runs, I hadn't taken my ATM card. I usually just stuffed the bills in my pants and shirt pockets, or in my carry-on or sometimes in my shoes and socks, and made the deposit when I got back to the island.

The bedroom had a full-size bed, a TV, a bathroom. There were bars on the one window. I figured this wasn't the first time the room was used as a prison cell. From the window, I could see the blue, purple and pink ocean during different times of the day. It was more than an overnight stay.

My story was that I had put the money from previous trips, $15,000, into what was called fixed-income bonds, held by an investment company and that I wasn't sure how long it would take to get the money out. (The money for the scholarship was really sitting in my savings account. I wouldn't touch it if they tightened a vise around my balls.) I was brought downstairs and allowed to make calls to get things rolling. These guys knew less about money market stuff than I did, and although I made the calls to the investment company, I faked the conversation. ("I'd like to sell off fifty shares of the preferred stock from Amalgamated Communications . . .") The guys on the other end of the line were wondering what the hell I was talking about.

It was Friday afternoon, so I told Papo a check for the $15,000 wouldn't be ready until Monday morning in the company's New York offices.

Papo shook his head, then took a very deep breath. Then he said to the others: "We got to feed this motherfucker over the weekend. I got business to take care of so make sure he don't leave this room."

Then he said to me: "We go to pick up the check in New York Monday and you sign it over to us. You got a gun to your head until the check is cashed."

"Right," I said.

"No check and you're goin' for another ride, only this one, you don't come back nowhere. You got that?"

I nodded, my mouth twitching.

I was brought back to the room and locked inside. My insides were locking themselves up again.

Why did I come up with that bullshit story about having the $15,000 in the money market, and I couldn't get it till Monday? Beats me. I suppose I was just playing for time until I figured out—whatever. Now I had this goddamn time under lock and key.

As I was looking through the window at the sky turning reddish gold and the ocean streaking purple, Papo drove off in his Mercedes.

We're in jeans and T-shirts and holding our shoes as we walk barefoot along the beach in the Condado at sunset. Laura is collecting purple-tinted seashells. I grab her and kiss her, deep. Her green-gray eyes get larger, then shut tight. I realize that I'd spend the rest of my life with her if she would agree.

Never to see her and hold her again. Never, never, never. She, never to live, love, experience again. What the fuck does that say about fairness, the justice in the world?

I sat back on the bed and started to read the Fanon book, but my eyes got heavy and I dozed.

I woke when the door was opened and a heavy paper bag was tossed at my feet.

"Dinner," said Junior. The bag had the McDonald's logo on it. "Happy Meal. Chicken McNuggets."

"Gracias."

Junior grunted. He looked at the book lying open next to me. "What you readin'?"

"*The Wretched of the Earth,*" I said. I showed him the cover.

"What's it about?"

"Colonialism. About people being held down by countries not their own and what they could do about it."

Junior's eyes suddenly got even smaller in his beefy face. "Politics is bullshit," he said like he was daring me to contradict him.

"Yeah, I suppose so. But . . ."

"Don't give me no 'buts.' You sound like that faggot professor I had at Boricua College, where I went for a year before I learned what was *real* in the world, and it wasn't reading about politics or any of that other bullshit. Anytime I would try to tell him about what was happening out there, he would say, 'Yes, but . . .'" Junior's voice went up high.

He pulled on his lower lip as he looked through me. Then he said: "There's one guy I like to read. Stephen King."

He's one of my favorite writers too," I said.

"You read *Cujo*, about that crazy fuckin' dog? It scared the shit out of me."

Junior, the tough enforcer for Papo, the big bruiser who knows what's real out in the world, scared by Stephen King. Beautiful!

"Did you read *Misery*?" I asked about my favorite King book.

"I seen the movie. Yeah, I read the book too."

"It's really about writing novels and what a writer goes through to . . ."

"Yeah, that's bullshit too. Eat your fuckin' dinner. Maybe the missing drugs will turn up in your next shit."

Junior left the room and locked the door. I guess he really didn't want to discuss literature.

I lay back on the bed, tapping the Saint John's medal around my neck. Laura gave me that medal, which was engraved in Spanish, *San Juan Bautista,* the patron saint of our city and island. For us, it wasn't so much a religious relic as an amulet recognizing our homeland. I looked down at the guy on the medal, his left hand in the air, his right hand holding a staff, a lamb at his feet.

I was trying like mad to figure out my next move. My insides were churning for a change.

I was hoping like hell that I didn't wind up like the saint on the medal.

FOUR

Ralph, a cabin boy, stands next to Grandfather Max, who leans over the rail of the freighter, smoking his corncob pipe. The smoke from the pipe whirls into the air then mixes with the vapor that rises from the smokestack of the ship. Ralph looks up at Max, at that lantern jaw, those sharp, high cheekbones and into those eyes, as green as the endless sea. The eyes, the sea, are flowing in and out of one another. Ralph asks where they are headed. "Are we going to look for my father, your son?"

"Nej," says Grandpa Max. "He is a drunken man. He is worth nothing. We go to look for your life—and for my death."

Ralph wakes from the recurring dream with tears behind his eyes. He flushes inside. Then he forgives himself. Somewhat.

Ralph's unforgivable sin against his father. Was that what gripped so tightly, sometimes almost suffocating?

His thin-mustached, usually drunken father, lying very soberly in his coffin, his sunken cheeks rouged. A ne'er-do-much-of-anything. He made mom suffer and pay for his drunkenness. At least Juan Camacho had a hands-off policy. He did, however, occasionally beat up on himself, actually slapping himself in the face, punching his own chest, where his heart was. His life slid down from once-respected Juan, the bookkeeper—teaching Ralph some tricks to remember the multiplication table, "Number 11 times up to 10, answer is always twins: 11, 22, 33, 44, 55, 66, 77, 88 and 99"—to Johnny the runner for bookies, to Juanito the bum. Toward the end, he slept in the streets. Mom, always two jobs at a time—in garment center factories during the week, cleaning other people's houses on the weekends. She refused welfare for the family. Young Ralph and Millie earning their keeps, delivering groceries, waiting tables, taking care of the infirm and the elderly.

Teenage Ralph serving pierogis and borscht at the Polish Center on Manhattan Avenue, bringing decks of cards to the old guys there. Andres, close to ninety, telling Ralph that Poland's greatest writer, Joseph Conrad, wrote in English. Gave him a paperback of Lord Jim.

Conrad, Literature with a capital L, inspiring Ralph to take to the eternal seas after the stinking paddies and suffocating jungles of Nam.

The calm and beautiful and raging and ugly sea. Ports and cities and people, often not as romantic as in the books. Just like life.

Use it, use it with the legend, the tragedy, of Max; use it to find the hidden core of what life is, by seemingly underplaying, but really exaggerating the imagined truth.

He'd start that next novel, about Swedish Grandfather Max, very soon. Max, who'd met *abuela* Concepción in Old San Juan when his ship was in port for two weeks, who married her after a whirlwind courtship and pledged to return after his next voyage to settle and start a business selling maritime goods. Who met his tragic fate on Borneo. In his short stay in Puerto Rico, Grandpa Max begat Juan, who sired Ralph. Ralph had Concepción's scrapbook: the yellowed, three-paragraph story from the *Sydsvenska Dagbladet*, a typewritten English-translation on a three-by-five card next to it:

> Malmo-native Max Johansson, 45, a son of Mr. and Mrs. Jurgen Johansson of 25 Sveavagen, has been killed in the jungles of South Kalimantan in Borneo by two brothers from the Southeast Asia island. They were charged with hacking him to death withparangs.
>
> The brothers were taken into custody immediately and remanded to prison in the capital city of Banjarmasin.
>
> Max Johansson was an officer aboard a merchant ship flying the flag of the United Kingdom. No one could say when and where the burial will take place.
>
> Authorities have given no immediate motive for the savage killing.

The official family story had Max, a womanizer, involved in the accidental death of a young woman who was related to the revenging brothers.

Besides Grandpa Max's sea-green eyes and Ralph's own earlier need to break away, did he inherit anything else from Max? If he imagined a life for Max, and solved the mystery of his death, on paper anyway, maybe he would discover more about himself. Is that why he wrote? No, yes. No! Who the hell knew—or cared? All he knew was that something was gripping him tight inside, just like before he wrote the first novel. The writing had eased the interior grip. But now it had clawed its way back.

His first book, *Man Alone*, was an autobiographical novel about growing up Nuyorican and sailing on freighters and being wounded and surviving as a rifleman with the 5th Infantry Division's 1st Brigade around Quang Tri. The book sold just a few hundred copies. But it gained notice in rarified academic circles after Harold Borenstein, a Rutgers University Professor of Ethnic Studies, wrote about it in a no-longer published literary quarterly. Borenstein said the novel was ripe with intimations of the Eternal Voyage, the Journey of the Hero over the Cosmic Sea, the Universal Return, the Spiritual Rebirth and the Collective Conscience of the Race.

Really? Ralph thought he had written a story of just one man learning about the vagaries of life in different places at a certain time. He accepted the offer of writer-in-residence at the University of Puerto Rico. Now—after leaving the island at the age of 10, "settling" in El Barrio, Brooklyn, Elizabeth, Jersey City—now, in the year 2000, after more than thirty-five years of exile, he was, so to speak, home.

Ralph checked the clock on the dresser beside the bed. Seven a.m. He would go to Richie's apartment in Río Piedras to try to catch his roommate. He also wanted to make a search of Richie's room. Sometimes, what's not in the room can be as telling as anything found.

Working for Confidential Investigations in Jersey City while writing his first novel, he had tracked down a missing student who faked his own kidnapping to demand $500,000 ransom from his millionaire dad. The plan began to unravel when Ralph searched the kid's Princeton dorm room and didn't find his copy of *War and Peace*.

Ralph had learned from several students about the new popularity of the Tolstoy classic, whose pages were cut away and replaced with stashes of pot. Ralph figured the kid took with him the one indispensable item while faking his abduction. After the father received a second ransom note postmarked Atlantic City, Ralph found the son at the Taj Mahal Hotel, anxiously waiting at poolside for his old man's payment.

Then there was the case of the pet crematorium in North Jersey. A cat owner who sent Molly, his dead, beloved tabby, to the location was beside himself when the urn he received from the crematorium was filled with what he learned was charred wood. So a sad-eyed Ralph brought "Charlie," his own deceased feline, to the crematorium. Actually what he gave them was a toy cat stuffed with raw hamburger meat, then frozen and wrapped in a white plastic bag. What he got back after paying the $250 fee, was a small green stone urn containing ashes and multiple bone samples. Since "Charlie" and the chopped meat both were boneless, and cremation experts said what should have been returned were simply a few metal pins and screws and a pinch of dust from the toy cat, the crematorium made a hefty out-of-court settlement with Molly's grieving owner.

Ralph was parked a block up from his house, on Calle Norzagaray, beside the Old City's centuries-old, blackened walls. Below the walls squatted the seaside slum of La Perla, its houses practically on top of one another, their roofs tar-papered green and black, the TV antennas crisscrossing the pastel blue sky. Beyond, the pulsating sun sparkled on the gulls-hovering sea.

He maneuvered back down Calle San Justo, past the restored, pastel pink and green and blue one-and two-story houses to Fortaleza Street, then around Plaza Colón and out of the Old City. Soon he was caught in the morning traffic jam. He didn't get to Richie's street until five minutes before nine. He checked the address he'd gotten from Richie's mother. The two-story house was in the middle of a block of other nondescript one- and two-story houses.

As Ralph was pulling into a parking spot across the street, a young guy came out from the front door of the house. He carried a backpack and wore sneakers, washed jeans, a white T-shirt and a blue baseball cap.

"Excuse me," Ralph shouted, "I'm looking for the roommate of Richie Pérez."

The fellow turned but continued walking backward. "I can't be late again for Legal Ethics. The professor actually locks the door. Whatta you want?"

"I want to talk to you. I'm looking for your friend."

"What for?"

"I'm trying to locate him. His mother is worried."

"Can we meet later? I can't miss any of my law school classes right now."

"When will you be free?"

"Noon. There's a Burger King across from the main gate. We can meet there."

Ralph got back in his car, drove to the campus, parked in his faculty spot and went to his office in the Humanities Building. He checked his snail mail and found a letter from the University's Office of Personnel asking for information for Social Security purposes. The stamped letter, sent from the building across the quad, came through the post office in San Juan. Couldn't someone in the office have phoned him, sent an email, yelled across the quad? They could have saved a stamp, an envelope, a sheet of paper, a tongue lick, a signature from the Personnel Director, a trip to the mailbox or post office, a clerk canceling, post-marking, bar-coding, sorting, a delivery by the mailman.

No phone messages. Just one email of note: a department meeting at 4:30 p.m. next Monday.

He decided to go to the University library for more research for his novel. What the hell did he know about Borneo where Grandpa Max met his end? He never got there in his Merchant Marine days.

As he started out the door to his office, bad luck brought him face-to-face with department head Hiram Rodríguez del Valle.

"I'm glad I caught you," said Rodríguez del Valle, blinking behind thick glasses.

Ralph tried, but couldn't get a smile going. His lips began to quiver; he couldn't fake it. He found this guy a huge pain in the ass.

Rodríguez del Valle looked his usual disheveled self. Thinning strands of gray-black hair were swirled atop his head. A flowery Sixties tie hung askew over a brown tweed jacket much too hot for the tropics. The image of the good-natured, absent-minded professor was at odds with the real Rodríguez del Valle, a pushy and punctilious schemer and university bureaucrat.

"You, of course, got the message about the meeting Monday? We have some very important business to go over, not the least of which will be the appointment of a new curriculum committee. Also, I'm very concerned about another matter: how we can get these kids from the U.S. mainland to, more or less, lose certain . . . umm, *attitudinal* prejudices they bring to their studies in this new academic discipline."

Ralph's "*attitudinal* prejudices" against Rodríguez del Valle had made him quit arguing with the department head, whose mind was as closed as his mouth was always open. He had been going out of his way to avoid the guy.

"I'm sure you know that not a hell of a lot of other universities have a Department of Nuyorican Studies," Rodríguez del Valle said. "We have to keep proving our worth to the administration. We have to keep the courses up-to-date with the latest requirements for accreditation. *Everyone* in this department has a responsibility to contribute. Too many of these kids are taking the courses because they believe they can slide through since what they will be taught in the classroom, they've already experienced in the ghettoes back in the states. This, of course, is not the idea at all. We want to rely on collected data as the basis for the discipline, rather than on anecdotal tales and hearsay, you know?"

Ralph grunted.

Rodríguez del Valle ignored the reaction. He usually ignored all reactions to what he said. The main thing was for him to listen to his own voice.

"Anyway, what I'm really concerned about right now is our committee work. Dean Salazar wants to see more results from the committees and I couldn't agree more. So, even though you have this special arrangement that allows you all the time in the world to continue 'creating,' while teaching just one course of your own making, I sincerely hope you will fulfill your responsibility to the Department and to the University and . . ."

"I'll see you at the meeting Monday." Ralph gave the department head a two-fingered salute as he took off down the corridor. He was reasonably sure that Rodríguez del Valle wanted him gone again after the semester. He'd deal with that when it happened.

He spent a couple of hours in the library, retrieving books about Borneo. He copied this from *Through Central Borneo: An Account of Two Years' Travel in the Land of Head-Hunters Between the Years 1913 and 1917,* by Carl Lumholtz:

> "It is extraordinary that such a revolting habit is practiced in
> a race the ethics of which otherwise might serve as a model
> for many so-called civilized communities, these natives being
> free to an unusual degree from the fault of appropriating
> what belongs to others and from untruthfulness. The fact that
> the Dayaks are amiable in disposition and inclined to timidity
> renders this phase of their character still more inexplicable.
> The inevitable conclusion is that they are driven to this outrage
> by religious influences and lose their self-control. siders, even
> if they have been staying a long time in the kampong, run a
> risk of losing their heads."

Ralph took notes. Were the killers Dayaks? Did Max lose his head to the "amiable" and "timid" headhunters?

Go figure people.

The roommate showed up outside the Burger King half an hour late. He apologized, explaining that he had to copy notes from a lecture he had previously missed.

Since there were long lines inside the restaurant and the last thing Ralph wanted was a greasy burger, he suggested they go to a nearby Cuban bakery, his treat. The roommate, who introduced himself as Mike Padilla, accepted.

Ralph explained his conversation with Richie's mother and her concern about Richie's whereabouts. Mike kept nodding while biting into his *cubano*.

"Richie tol' m' 'bou' you," he said while trying to down the food in his mouth. "You his fav'rit prof."

Ralph waited for Mike to digest. "Do you know where he is?"

Mike shook his head. "He told me last week that he was going away for a couple of days, but would be back for classes by Monday. What's today? Thursday? I haven't heard from him since."

"He didn't say anything, give you any hint where he might be going?"

"That's his business. If he wanted me to know, I'm sure he would have told me."

"You didn't ask him?"

"Yeah, I asked him."

"And?"

"And he said he couldn't tell me."

"Has he ever done this before?"

"He's taken off on weekends, just as I have. We've only been sharing the apartment for a few months. I mean we're close, but not *that* close where we know all about each other's lives, you know? Of course, I know about that girl, his girlfriend, Laura. He blamed himself for convincing her to join the protest that day. He felt he should have taken the cop's bullet."

Mike bit into his *cubano* again and Ralph waited while he chewed and washed it all down with a Pepsi in a huge plastic cup. After several deep gulps of soda, he continued: "O.K., I'll tell you this. You might say this is circumstantial evidence, but several weeks ago Richie said he was looking for a way to arrange it so that people would always remember Laura and what she stands for."

"What do you think that means?"

Mike shrugged, then nodded, as though deciding to let Ralph into something he might not be aware of. "Laura has become a martyr for all of us who want the Navy to stop bombing Vieques, where people are trying to live their lives. We want Puerto Rico to be its own country, you know?"

"So you think his trip has something to do with . . . what, something connected to Laura?"

"I plead *nolo contendere,*" the law student said.

Ralph asked if Mike wouldn't mind going back to the apartment so he could have a look at Richie's room.

"Let's see, I got a two o'clock in Commercial Arbitration. Could we meet back at the apartment after the class?"

Ralph looked at his watch. "It was already two. "O.K., we'll meet back there at three."

"*Chévere,* good deal," said Mike Padilla. "See you then."

Ralph ordered another ink-black Cuban coffee. The lunch crowd was emptying out, but several burly businessmen-types were at the bar, sucking on cigars and, with thick fingers. daintily picking up demitasse cups of the powerful coffee. Ralph went to a nearby, empty table, collected a copy of today's paper and brought it back to his table. Vieques led the news again. It's an issue that won't go away until the Navy does, Ralph thought.

> VIEQUES, Puerto Rico (AP)—Hundreds of demonstrators on this small island off the east coast of Puerto Rico were removed early yesterday from the Navy's target range by 200 FBI agents, 100 U.S. marshals, 1,000 Marines, and local police SWAT teams.
>
> In reaction, protestors paralyzed traffic in San Juan. Demonstrators also blocked entrances to Fort Buchanan Army Base in San Juan.
>
> University of Puerto Rico students say they hope to find a way to shut down the university in protest.
>
> The demonstrations have been going on for over a year, since an errant Navy bomb killed David Sanes Rodríguez, a civilian employee of the Navy and a Vieques resident, in April 1999.
>
> The Navy owns two-thirds of Vieques.
>
> A Puerto Rican government report says the military exercises over almost 60 years have caused serious environmental harm and stunted the economy.
>
> The Navy denies any environmental damage and says its live-fire training on Vieques is essential to save lives in U.S. conflicts.

> Many of those arrested yesterday remain in jail. They have refused to post bail saying they don't recognize the jurisdiction of federal courts in Puerto Rico.

At 3:15, Ralph was back at Richie's house. Mike was there by 3:30. There seemed nothing unusual about Richie's half of the large second-floor room, which resembled college students' rooms just about anywhere, but with a Puerto Rican accent. There were posters and pictures on the wall—Che, of course; Puerto Rican revolutionary leaders Betances and Albizu Campos; blowup photos of Roberto Clemente leaning on a bat and Yankees slugger Bernie Williams taking a swing. There were a couple of New York Yankees caps and baseball gloves on wall hooks and there were books and CDs and vinyl LPs on wooden boards lying across cement bricks. Richie's literary interests seemed to lean to political bios (Che, Gandhi, Malcolm X) and to novels by Stephen King. His musical tastes tended to salsa and Afro-Cuban jazz. Underwear, shirts, jeans, shorts, socks, sneakers were in ample supply in drawers and in the closet. His desk was very neat. Next to a computer were a glass-encased baseball with autographs of several Yankees on it and a framed photo of Richie—narrow, handsome face, olive-skinned with fairly long sideburns and the shadow of a goatee—with his arm around a girl, pale and beautiful with large soulful eyes.

"Laura Rosario," Mike said.

Ralph looked at the photo for a long time.

Exiting from a class in the Humanities building, seeing Richie struggling with police. Helping him get out of the way of the gunfire. The girl crumpled lifeless on the walk in the quad. The memorial service on campus, the funeral in the Old City. Richie in confused mourning.

A manila folder sat beneath the photo frame. Ralph picked it up, flipped through it. He opened the desk drawers. Paper clips, scissors, tape, print paper, manila folders, clasp envelopes, etc.

"Do you know Richie's password for the computer?"

Mike shook his head. "We don't share stuff like that," he said.

"Is his desk usually this neat?"

"Yeah, he's a neatness nut."

"Anything missing that's usually here?"

"Not that I can see. Everything looks about the same," Mike said, giving the room a perfunctory once over.

Ralph went through the papers again in the manila folder under the photo. There were newspaper clippings, reports, propaganda leaflets and other material on the Navy's maneuvers in Vieques. A recent newspaper article said an investigation showed the mortality rate on Vieques was 34 percent higher than in Puerto Rico, 50 percent higher from cancer deaths, 40 percent higher from heart disease. A 57-year-old fisherman, who had lived on the small island all his life, a non-smoker who contracted lung cancer last year, said: "The Navy is killing American citizens in Vieques." The quote was highlighted in red.

At the bottom was a flyer announcing that the Hotel Employees and Restaurant Employees Union (HERE) was planning a strike in several of the island's hotels and casinos. The flyer was a couple of years old and the strike had come and gone.

Did Mike know why Richie had that flyer?

Mike shrugged, put his palms up. "Richie worked one summer busing tables at a restaurant at the Caribe Hilton if that's any help."

Ralph gave Mike his cell number and asked him to call if he got any word from or about Richie.

"Sure thing."

The union's island representative worked out of a small office in a concrete two-story building just off traffic-heavy Highway Two. The young fellow said he'd had the job for just the past few months and couldn't recall a visit from anyone named Richie Pérez. He referred Ralph to Pedro Feliciano, the retired union leader of HERE who now lived in Orlando.

He went to get Feliciano's telephone number. But after a twenty-minute search through a Rolodex and several file cabinets, he came up empty.

"I'm really sorry. Lucy, our secretary, would have it. But she's in New York and won't be back for a couple of days."

"That's O.K.," Ralph said. "I'll track Pedro Feliciano down."

"Good luck. If you need to, give me a call in the next few days and I'll put you in touch with Lucy."

Ralph left the building where other labor unions, once occupying large spaces in the heart of the city, were now located. Outside, the smell from the nearby municipal dump hung putridly in the still, hot air. Ralph got into his car and was just in time for the five p.m. *tapón*. The air-conditioning kicked in, halfway. He'd have to get it fixed before the summer heat came on full strength.

There were four Pedro Felicianos and two P. Felicianos listed in the Orlando area. The operator said she could only give Ralph three numbers. He called information again and got the other three. One Pedro was never home, another's phone was always busy, the other two Pedros said they were not the retired labor leader. The two P's were Pablo and Paula. Pablo was the son of a Pedro that Ralph already had spoken to. Paula just moved to Orlando from the island and knew of no other Felicianos in Florida.

Ralph dialed several more times, leaving his home number for the Pedro who was not answering. He kept getting a busy signal on the other Pedro's line. He decided to call it a night.

The next morning, one of the Pedro Felicianos still hadn't answered. But the other Pedro Feliciano, whose phone had been busy, did. In a rasping foggy voice that faded in and out, he said he was the Pedro Felicano who had spent thirty-five years in the Puerto Rico labor movement.

Ralph introduced himself as a professor at the University of Puerto Rico looking for a missing student, at the request of the student's mother.

Feliciano said he was a retired widower who had moved to Florida to be close to his daughter and grandchildren. He now had plenty of time on his hands, even though he could still put in a full day's work. He hadn't gone so long without working since he was twelve or thirteen. Before he became union leader, he worked for many years as a croupier at the Caribe Hilton. Now he missed the action. He was thinking of getting a cashier's job at one of the restaurants in town.

Did Sr. Feliciano know a Richie Pérez, a University student who worked for a summer at the Hilton hotel?

"Call me Pete." Feliciano broke into several seconds of a hacking cough. "I don't know what the hell *that* was, I haven't smoked in three years. Anyway, what can I do for you?"

"I'm trying to track down a young fellow named Richie Pérez. I found some information about the union among his papers."

"Pérez? Richie Pérez? "

"He may have contacted you after his girlfriend was killed during a demonstration at the University."

"The thing at the University where the young girl was killed? Yeah, I remember that. Those bastards! Don't know how to control themselves. That strike at the Holiday Inn in Isla Verde a couple of years ago? The Riot Squad sent a dozen of our members to the hospital. The bastards even shot two!"

Another coughing fit, then: "Yeah, that kid came to see me, about a year ago. He said he worked with our union at the Caribe Hilton. He wanted to talk to me about that girl at the University. You know about the girl being shot, right?"

"Do you remember just why Richie made the visit?"

"Sure. It was about that girl. She was his girlfriend, right? Yeah, he wanted to know if we could contribute money for a health clinic on Vieques that would be named after her. He wanted to raise money for the clinic to be named in her honor so the people will always remember her and why she died. That's what he said. A nice kid, but sort of, you know, innocent, about how things work. I told the kid that the union was having trouble meeting its own pension plan, maybe he should look for the money in other places too, or scale down his project. He left, saying he would look into it. But I could tell, he was disappointed and pissed. But a health clinic? You know how much that would cost? He sure as hell didn't.

"Anyway, he came back to see me just before I retired to tell me he was working on a scholarship named after the girl and asked how much the union could contribute. So I told him we would be a sponsor of the scholarship and pledge a certain amount provided he could show how much he had collected. He said he had been trying local businesses and charities without any luck, but he finally found a way to get more money but didn't want to say how, or from where. He said we'd hear from him soon. Lucy, she works at the union office, knows about what happened. I told him to contact her. I don't know if he has."

Ralph thanked Pete Feliciano, who said: "Call again, anytime, for whatever."

Ralph called the HERE office after a couple of days. Lucy said the last she had heard from Richie was some weeks ago. Richie told her he would soon have $20,000 to get the scholarship underway. It would be for students studying Latin American and Puerto Rican literature, which Laura had wanted to teach.

Where had Richie gone? Where was he getting that kind of money? Why hadn't he returned yet?

Ralph would damn well find out.

FIVE

Nothing happened over the weekend, except for the pictures in my head of a multi-bullet-holed me lying just off the turnpike. I got Dunkin' Donuts breakfasts and more McDonald's Happy Meals. I forced myself to take a couple of bites. I finished the Fanon book. The colonial mentality, whether in Black Africa or Algeria or Puerto Rico, it's the same, only with a different style, if you know what I mean. Fanon is all for violence to fight colonialism and to bring about a new man evolving in a new society. Good stuff. But not that good. To be honest, I'm still trying to figure out the best way for Puerto Rico to come into its own.

Papo came back to the Jersey house Sunday night. He told me that on Monday we would all meet in New York, and the check better be ready or "you ain't gonna see Tuesday, or any other days."

I told him: "My Mom was expecting to hear from me days ago. I usually call her every day or every other day and she's probably worried as hell. You know how Puerto Rican moms are. So could I just call her to let her know that I'm O.K.?"

My motives were just that. I didn't want to worry poor Mom. I hadn't talked to her for over a week. "How old are you?" Papo asked.

"Nineteen," I said, reducing my age a year.

"When I was nineteen I was killin' fuckin gooks in Nam," he said, shaking his head at my arrested development. "O.K., one call to *Mami,* in the morning. Real fast, thirty seconds."

"Gracias."

Early the next morning, Chucho, the little jerk, brought my cell phone to my room and stayed there while I made the call. The anxiety in my mother's voice hurt. I couldn't say too much, except to let her know I was OK and would try to call again soon.

"*Ay, m'ijo*, why do you do this to me? Worry me like this?"

"I'm really sorry, Mom. Please don't worry. Something really important came up."

"I was so worried that I asked Professor Camacho to help me find out what had happened to you."

Jesus! "No, he doesn't have to do anything. I'll be back soon."

"But where are you?"

"I'll call back soon and . . ." I pushed the off button, hoping Mom would think we got disconnected. Junior yelled for Chucho to come downstairs and make some coffee for Papo.

"*Voy, voy,*" Chucho said.

He forgot to take the cell phone back. I hurriedly called Mike Padilla.

"It's me, Richie. Hey, I can't talk long. You gotta do me a gigantic favor."

"I'm listening," Mike said. "But make it fast. I got Legal Ethics in five minutes and . . ."

"Remember the guy I told you about, Manny El Bronx? You got to go to Llorens tonight after midnight, by the community center, he'll be there, and tell that sonovabitch to call Papo and straighten out a problem I got up here with some people in New York. It's about a delivery that wasn't filled, they think I'm keeping it from them, so they're holding me. He's got to explain to them what happened. He'll know what you're talking about."

"Whatever the hell *that* is."

"Don't worry about it. Just tell him to call Papo, pronto! O.K.? I gotta go now."

"Yeah, but . . ."

"O.K., I gotta hang up."

I thought Mike would get a hold of Manny and Manny would make that call before tomorrow and everything would be cleared up.

That's how fucked up my thinking was.

After a couple of minutes, Chucho came back to the room. "The phone," he said.

"Yeah?"

"Give me your fuckin cell phone, asshole, or you're really gonna be in deep shit." He clicked open his switchblade like he was getting ready for a rumble.

I gave him the cell phone.

I spent most of the rest of the day thinking about how I was going to pull myself out of the shit I already was sinking into.

We moved out early the next morning. Chucho took me by the arm while he snapped his switchblade open and shut a couple of times and pushed me in the back of a red Ford Mustang. He got in next to me. Junior drove. I had a terrific headache, which, I realized, was the least of my problems.

The vise was tightening again on my kidneys and liver and pancreas and the other stuff in there. I still had no idea what I was going to do before or after we got to New York.

We sped back into the Pine Barrens. The sun spread over the two-lane road that cut between the dense forest of stunted pine trees. The pain in my head was telling me to forget the pains in my stomach.

The forest seemed weird and mysterious, even in the daytime. I could see them dumping me here. From living in Bayonne, I also knew about The Jersey Devil. The Jersey Devil supposedly was born in the Pine Barrens a couple hundred years ago and, supposedly, is still around, freaking out residents. It has horns growing from the top of its head and claws sprouting from its fingertips, not to mention leathery bat wings and hair and feathers all over its body. It has glowing bright red eyes and a twisted, snarling face. Right after its birth, it killed its own mother, If only there was some way I could call up the Jersey Devil to attack Junior and Chucho and carry me off. Which might be the only way, I was thinking, I could get out of this.

Damn! If things had only worked out, I could have had enough to start up the scholarship for the next year. If they wanted to know at the University, I'd tell them that the money was an inheritance from an uncle who died in California. If they wanted proof, I'd tell them, forget it, and set up the scholarship through the Federation of Pro-Independence Students. Then, with my master's in Latin American and Caribbean History in a couple of years, I'd be teaching somewhere, and I'd be able to keep funding the scholarship with part of my salary. Once the Laura Rosario Scholarship in Hispanic and Puerto Rican Literature got going, I'd have picked up contributions from unions, foundations, and other places.

I still see her eyes at night, when I go to bed. She's in my dreams too. We're down by the shore, it's a beautiful sunny day. But then clouds suddenly slide in and it becomes overcast and as I reach out to her, her body turns to mist and my arms go through her and she shrinks and disappears into the foam rolling back into the ocean.

She was lying there, like a broken doll. The cops said they acted in self-defense because shots were being fired in their direction. A couple of them were suspended, but are now back on the force. I blame myself more than I blame the cops. They were just some *pendejos* put there to keep the U.S. rule over Puerto Rico. I more or less convinced Laura to go with me to the protest. It was part of our schedule for the day: morning classes, lunch at Kentucky Fried Chicken, the demonstration, then *The Battle of Algiers* at the University's movie club.

She had such smooth skin. She looked like a kid until you got close enough to see that she swelled in the right places. Those large, restless eyes seemed to always be questioning what was happening around her. I fell for her the moment we met in a Spanish Lit class where we were studying *Don Quixote.* I kissed her that evening, outside her dorm room, after we saw Bunuel slice into an eyeball in *Un Chien Andalou.* We spent weekends at the beach in Boquerón, where we swam in the clear, calm, blue bay and ate small, sweet oysters bought from street vendors, and made love in the tiny room we rented in the rickety hotel that jutted out over the bay.

She said she loved me, but I think I loved her more because there were more things about her to love.

She was small, but her heart was huge. She lived like a poor student because she kept giving things away— money, clothes, jewelry; anything—to other students and to street people. I saw her take off a beautiful vintage cameo brooch and pin it on the blouse of one of her girlfriends, who was admiring it. No explanations, she just did it. She was so honest, and a lot more mature than me. We were at a party in Old San Juan once and some gringo business guy was coming on to her and even though she saw me starting to get angry, she kept talking to him, laughing at his stupid jokes, seeming interested in what he told her about his job running a pharmaceutical factory out in Barceloneta. When the evening ended and we were our way back to Río Piedras, she saw I was pissed.

"Why are you angry?" she asked

"Because you were showing so much attention to that guy," I said. "You came to the party with me."

She took her bottom lip between her fingers and nodded. Then she said: "Number one: I love you. I've told you that. If anything changes I'll definitely let you know. Number two, that fellow was a newcomer to the island and I wanted to make him feel comfortable. Number three, we're not married, and I don't think we should be yet.

That means our individual behavior is our own responsibility and since our shared values, and our moral actions, seem to remain intact, I don't see any reason why either of us should feel we have to hold back on our natural inclinations, as long as they are rational and reasonable, since we both know that we are the most important and cherished beings in each other's lives.

"Also," she said, "I love you, so kiss me."

Which I did, as soon as we exited the very crowded Number One bus in front of the University.

So from that day or night, on, we understood one another. Rather, I was beginning to understand Laura, since she already knew most of what made me, me.

She always thought about how her actions would affect other people. When you meet someone who really does unto others as she would have them do unto her, it makes you believe there is such a thing as being touched by the grace of God. She made me a better person.

Was I idolizing her? Was she really that good a person?

Yeah, she was.

We got onto the Turnpike, Junior driving mostly with one hand while constantly answering his cell phone with the other. Most of what he had to say was said in few words: "*Si, si; no, no; no me digas; bueno; mierda; okay.*"

Then I heard him say: "Broadway? The statue of the bull? Near Wall Street? Yeah, yeah, don't worry, I'll find it."

I had told them that the financial company was on Wall Street. Should I dash out of the car as soon as we got to Wall Street? Would they shoot to kill in the crowded lunchtime crowd? Instead of the bullet hitting me, would it pierce through the head or heart of some young woman just out of college trying to learn the financial markets?

Damn! I was paralyzed!

We whizzed past the thick-leaved and willowy trees, the high walls along the sides of the road built to keep out noise from the surrounding communities, the exits leading to farmland and countryside New Jersey. A billboard announced, with a picture of the book: **"The Holy Bible. Inspired! Absolute! Final!"** We had not yet hit the sci-fi towers and smoky refineries around Linden, Elizabeth, and Newark.

Chucho kept nodding off beside me, his head jerking in all directions before popping up again. His hair was tied back in a ponytail. I would have loved to have grabbed that little tail to smash his head against a window and have jumped out of the car—if we weren't going ninety miles an hour.

Then, about halfway to New York, we began to slow down and Junior announced: "I need some coffee."

Wha?" said Chucho, suddenly sitting up.

"I said I'm gonna stop for some coffee."

"Yeah, I got to piss so bad I can taste it," Chucho said. "Let's make it at the next rest stop."

We soon saw a sign for the Joyce Kilmer Service Area. Junior followed the off ramp and we parked to the left near the entrance.

"Take him to the bathroom with you," Junior said. "I'll get us coffee. You want some coffee?" he asked me.

"Yeah, thanks."

The sun was gone and smoky gray clouds were passing overhead like the Jersey refineries were just around the corner.

Chucho snapped his switchblade open as we entered the men's room. He showed me the blade and tucked the knife into his belt. There were three or four other guys pissing into the dozen or so urinals. Someone was gaseously dumping in one of the several stalls. Chucho went to the urinal nearest the exit and directed me to the one next to him. Pulling his head back, crinkling up his face and closing his eyes, he let out sounds of satisfaction as he pissed heavily into the urinal.

My chance. Now, or maybe never.

I jumped behind Chucho, grabbed a handful of his mullet, pushed his head hard against the metal pipes above the urinal. He screamed and turned halfway. I punched him in the face. He crumpled onto the floor, alongside streams of his piss and the blood from his nose.

The other guys at the urinals issued "What the fuck!"s. The water flushed inside the occupied stall. Chucho had a hand over his face and was moaning. Zipping up, I scooted around him and out the door. I tried to walk quietly across the restaurant area to the front door.

Junior was headed to the station that held the sugar, napkins and plastic utensils. He was carrying three cups of coffee in a cardboard holder. He spotted me and called out. As I took off again, he stalled for a minute, looked down at the coffee and creased up his face, like the cups were telling him something he didn't want to hear; then he dropped the holder with the cups onto the floor and dashed after me.

I ran out the front door and toward the gas station where cars clogged the lanes. Junior took off after me, stopped with one foot in the air, then turned and ran back for his car. It was raining, hard.

I shot between the cars, knocking into an attendant carrying a hose to a waiting vehicle.

"Whoa! What's up?" said the guy, who was in a rain jacket and hood.

I ran toward a football field-sized area for trucks and buses. The hard rain was turning into a torrential downpour, the drops skipping along the concrete like colorless jumping beans. Over my shoulder, I saw Junior's Ford Mustang maneuvering around the lines of cars refilling at the pumps. Praying he hadn't seen me, I crawled under the cab of a parked sixteen-wheeler.

Junior drove by the trucks and the buses. The Mustang slowly circled the area. It stopped once, twice, Junior got out, looked in some of the buses, under some of the trucks—thank God not under the one I was under--then drove back to the front of the building and parked again. He went back into the building, and I rolled out from under the cab and dashed across a grassy area leading to the exit from the service area. .

Maneuvering along the edge of the Turnpike, I had to hop across a metal road barrier. I was on an emergency lane that was backed by one of those high anti-noise walls. I ran far down the emergency lane until the wall disappeared by an overpass. Some of the cars beeped their horns as they sped and splashed past me. It was coming down in torrents.

Climbing over another low metal barrier, I landed in a quasi-swamp bordering the roads. I lurched through the mud until I reached a wooded area. I slipped along and scooted over logs and pushed through twisted, low-hanging branches of willow and oak trees. Half my khakis were soaked black from the swamp and my t-shirt was sticking to my back. But "civilization" was just a couple of hundred yards ahead, where several small houses stood.

I had no cell phone, no credit card, no cash, nothing. But I was still in one piece and I was free to go . . . someplace.

SIX

The call came just as Ralph was waking. It was Mrs. Pérez. "I just heard from Richie," she said, excitedly, and with a note of unease.

"He told me he was O.K. When I asked him where he was, he wouldn't tell me and he couldn't say when he was coming back to the island. I started crying"—as she was now—"and he said, 'Oh, Mom, don't worry,' and I told him, How could I not worry? Then I told him I talked to you and you were helping me and he said to tell you please not to do anything to try to find him, he was all right, he'd call again, and then the line went dead."

"How did he sound?"

"Oh, I don't know. The same, but not really."

"How different?"

"I don't know!" She broke down again.

"All right, Mrs. Pérez. Let me know as soon as you hear from him again."

"I'm not leaving my house. I'll call in sick and stay by the phone until I hear his voice again."

Richie apparently was still in one piece, somewhere.

"I'm bringing up the matter for the good of all, especially for the members of the curriculum committee. It pains me to say this," Chairman Rodríguez del Valle told Ralph, looking more self-righteous than pained, "but I've had complaints from faculty in our own Humanities Department. As I'm sure you know, I have questioned your choice of course material, and now I have complaints from other professors who believe that not only are you not qualified to teach the classics, especially on a graduate level, but that the works you have used in your course contradict the description and goals of Nuyorican Studies. We are tasked with establishing a curriculum of study that we recognize as the Puerto Rican Diaspora, the mass movement from the Island to the States, and back to the Island, and we want to establish this department as contributing to the University's intellectual and academic standards. In other words, the courses should be at once relevant to and aimed at enhancing the curriculum, based on recognized studies rather than on anecdotal 'evidence' and hearsay, as offered by the students, themselves.

"I realize there is nothing the department could do right now, since your contract calls for you to prepare your own course, but I bring it up as a sort of guide for the work of the Department's curriculum committee as its members wrestle with which courses we should retain, which we should jettison and which we should incorporate in future semesters."

Rodríguez del Valle smiled around the long table in the Humanities Building conference room. The department's one other full professor, Ray Gutiérrez, its two assistant professors and two lecturers—looked everywhere except at the chairman. Assistant Professor Myra Fuentes, who taught a course in Nuyorican poetry, had a hurt look on her face, as though the chairman's critique was aimed at her (She had made some comparisons in her class between stateside women Puerto Rican poets and the Ancient Greek poet Sappho). Gutiérrez, a Harvard-educated economics professor, who taught a course on the Puerto Rican migration and capitalism, looked dejected.

"Any questions before we call it a night?" asked Rodríguez del Valle.

All eyes were on Ralph. He knew the sonovabitch was getting it all on record—a secretary was taking the minutes—so he could, at the least, get Ralph out of the department for good, since Ralph had no academic credentials, except for a few night-school courses at the City University of New York, and had consistently ignored all advice of the chairman. Ralph said nothing. He just wanted to get the hell out of the room and get home.

"Well," said the chairman, "I suppose that brings to a close . . ."

"I'd like to make a comment," said middle-aged, salt-and-pepper-bearded, tenured professor Gutiérrez.

He took off his black-rimmed glasses and tucked them in the top pocket of his white guayabera, looked down at the desk in front of him and rubbed his chin, as though gathering his thoughts. Then he looked up and addressed his audience:

"I have several students who have taken Ralph Camacho's classes and they all have nothing but good things to say about those classes. You see, there is a whole world outside of academia. There are writers and artists, among others, who have delved into the depths of that world. They have come up with insights and understandings that may have bypassed others residing within their gilded academic boxes. Because of their comprehension, these people have an intuitive grasp of mankind's great thoughts and feelings. They are more than capable of igniting the spark of learning in the young. For the lucky few, that spark will burn throughout their lives. In other words, I see nothing wrong with, and a hell of a lot right about Ralph Camacho teaching the classics and giving a touchstone to kids from El Barrio and the Bronx to relate their own lives in their own ways to the lives and adventures of heroes, ancient and literary."

Silence.

Ralph gave Gutiérrez, whom he just knew from perfunctory greetings, a nod of appreciation. What could he say? Here was an economics professor outside the gilded academic box.

Gutiérrez nodded, unsmiling, in return.

"All right," said Rodríguez del Valle, "now that we've all had our say, we'll wrap it up."

As Ralph was getting into his car to drive home, his cell phone rang. Tere, who sounded happily frazzled, told him the head of Legal Services had just called to ask if she would join the staff and could she come to a meeting that evening. So would he bring home a pizza for a late dinner?

"That's great news! I'll also bring home a bottle of champagne."

O.K., sweetie. I'll see you."

It's about time, thought Ralph. This was what Tere was hoping and praying for. She had quit the corporate-lawyer track in New York because . . . well, "Why make the rich richer? Is that what I want to spend my life doing? I don't think so."

So, among other things, this would mean that he'd be picking up Diana from school, cooking dinners and, when he started on the novel, either hiring someone to take his two-hour afternoon chores when he spelled Tere at the Wishy Washy Laundromat (named by daughter Diana) or just closing it down. Tere had bought the business from her Aunt Felicia's cousin Paula to supplement Ralph's meager teaching salary. Maybe Doña Juana, the widow who lived down the block and worked for them part-time, would like to run the place full time.

His next novel: Max, an old salt, mentors a young protagonist, a kid who goes to sea for the first time. Their adventures together. Surrogate father, surrogate son. The young guy learns hard lessons about life, about character, about fate.

Why can't he start the novel?

Just sit down and write the damn thing!

Tere came home as Diana was getting ready for bed.

"They want me to start next week. The salary is about the same as we make from the laundromat. But I'll be a lawyer again."

"Great!"

"Yeah, we'll be on easy street—just like where I was born and raised, " Flatbush Brooklyn-native Tere said, her deep brown eyes sparkling in her thin and lovely face.

"O.K.," Ralph said. "You'll be the Dorothy Day of the legal profession."

"I'll do it, for the love of humanity."

"For whoever and whatever you love."

Tere and Ralph kissed. Ralph popped open the champagne. They drank two glasses apiece, then went to bed and made love. His wife's toughness turned to a half-growling need, then to a sweeping tenderness that Ralph realized only the truly generous could bestow.

Once again a wakeup call, at seven a.m. It wasn't Mrs. Pérez. It was Mike Padilla, Richie's roommate.

"I'm sorry to call you so early, Professor Camacho. But I got a call from Richie yesterday. I couldn't call you before because I had a paper due, like three days ago, on Comparative Law: Conflict and Unification."

"What's going on? Where is he?"

"He said he was moving around. He said I had to do him a great favor."

"What's that?"

"Well, he said he made some sort of delivery for a guy he knows in San Juan. Then he said the people he made the delivery to said it wasn't all there. He said they think he took the part that's missing, so they're not letting him go."

"What are we talking about?"

"I'm not sure."

What the hell—a *delivery*?

"Are we talking about drugs? Was Richie delivering drugs?"

"He didn't say."

"Did you ask him?"

"Yeah, but he said he couldn't tell me."

"Where does that leave us?" Ralph was rapidly getting pissed. Richie, a drug mule?

"I don't know, sir. The reason I called you is because you said if I hear anything, I should let you know. Which I'm doing."

"All right, what else?"

"He wanted me to see this guy, his name is Manny el Bronx, to tell him about the delivery. It sounded to me like he was in trouble, like if it didn't get fixed, like, maybe, who knows? Richie said the guy hangs out in Llorens Torres. Everyone knows him there, and maybe I could go out to the project and find Manny el Bronx and tell him he has to contact them to tell them he wouldn't—something or other because then the phone went dead. So I'm freaked out. I don't know what the hell I should do. I got a test coming up tomorrow in Business Torts and I haven't studied, and if I flunk this one, I could fail the course, which would mean . . ."

"All right," said Ralph. "Thanks for calling." He hung up.

Richie, a mule. He couldn't believe it. Such a smart kid doing such a dumb thing!

Manny el Bronx in Llorens Torres, the huge drug-infested housing project in San Juan.

Beautiful!

After midnight was the time to catch Manny El Bronx in Llorens Torres. That's what the two young guys drinking beer and leaning on the fender of a beat-up Chevy in the housing project told Ralph. It was high noon and the sun blazed off the top floors of the four-story concrete apartment buildings and it burnished the tops of the junked cars sitting on ragged lawns between the buildings. It seared the grass and sizzled the smell of garbage in the air and heated the breeze that brought in a trace of salt spray from the ocean several blocks away. It nearly scalded the balding spot on the top of Ralph's head.

"He don't start supervising and selling until the heavy traffic comes after midnight," said one of the guys.

"He's usually at the *punto* right by the community center," said the other. "He likes to shoot baskets in the court outside there when he ain't workin', which nowadays ain't almost never because business is really good."

The two guys, both skinny, with scarred arms and darkly circled eyes, slapped hands.

"Does he live here, in the project?" Ralph asked.

"Nah, why would he live in this shithole when he makes all the dinero?" the first guy asked.

"He used to live here, but now he's got a house in Bayamón," said the other.

Did they know where in Bayamón? They shook their heads.

Ralph thanked the junkie twins and drove off. He passed the apartment-crowded buildings with infant-to-old-age clothing drying across the tiny balconies and flags of political parties that never kept their promises drooping from windows. Stripped cars were junked up on khaki-colored parched lawns. The sprawling housing project was home to some 37,000 residents, more populated than several of the island's towns.

At home that evening, Ralph tried to convince Diana, who had just finished a portrait of Snugs, her guinea pig, that Picasso's many-faced women had not been painted under the influence of pot.

"Still," she said, "if I'm going to be an artist, shouldn't I try to experience all sorts of things, including pot? I'm mature for my age. You said so."

"Not that mature," Ralph said. "Become a real artist first."

She nodded slowly, wisely, blinking those big dark brown eyes. "Yeah, O.K."

Why did he think that his 13-year-old daughter was humoring him?

After dinner, they watched a NOVA program about a bee colony, where he learned that the honey bees' wings stroke 200 beats per second, which causes the buzzing, and that honey is the only food that includes everything necessary to sustain life and that it contains an antitoxin that improves brain functioning. More bee colonies could help us all get out of the mess we're in, Ralph thought.

Then came the local news, highlighting still another drug "massacre" that claimed five lives in a roadside bar.

At midnight, he was ready for his visit to Manny El Bronx. Tere was far from overjoyed.

"*Vaya con Dios,*" she said, "and maybe with a .38 too. Do you really have to go? I don't think . . ."

"Don't worry," Ralph said. "I'll be careful. I still have to finish folding Don Freddo's corsets and bras tomorrow for his transvestite show at the Parrot Club."

Tere smiled, sort-of.

Ralph drove into Llorens Torres, behind a red Jag, which trailed a black Mercedes. As they entered through the gate, some guys at the entrance spoke into cell phones. The cars ahead slowed as they reached the community center, a nondescript two-story brick building. Windows rolled down as young guys ambled over to the cars, dug into shirt and jacket and pants pockets and exchanged plastic bags for the twenties, fifties, hundreds.

When Ralph drove up, a kid who couldn't have been more than fourteen or fifteen put an arm on the roof of the Toyota. The kid, wearing a New York Yankees cap with the lid to the side, raised his eyebrows and jerked his head up in silent questioning.

"Watcha want?"

"I need to speak to Manny el Bronx," Ralph said.

"Who you?"

"A friend of a friend."

The kid kept looking at Ralph. Ralph looked less friendly at the kid. The kid pulled his arm off the roof, turned and went across the street to the front of the community center, where guys with sideways-and-backward-wearing baseball caps were on cell phones and walkie-talkies.

The kid pointed to Ralph's car. A guy dressed in black looked over and put up a hand like he was saying he'd be there in a minute. He was talking to someone who was talking to someone else on a cell. The two shook hands as the second guy kept talking into the phone and the hatless fellow in black strutted over to Ralph's car.

"Hey, amigo, what can I do for you?" He leaned into the window, smiling, at ease, as though he and Ralph were old buddies. The guy had tight wavy black hair and a pock-marked face. His silky black shirt was opened to his stomach and buttoned at the cuffs Around his neck, he wore a gold cross on a gold chain. His black pants were neatly pressed.

"I'm looking for Manny El Bronx."

"Yeah?"

"I'm here about Richie Pérez. I'm a professor at the University and he's one of my students."

"Yeah?"

I've heard from Richie. He seems to be in some sort of trouble and says only Manny El Bronx can help him."

"Verdad?" The guy, who Ralph was sure was Manny, kept smiling. His left eye twitched almost imperceptibly.

"He said he was being accused of coming up short on a delivery."

Manny's eyes shot wide open. "Really? Jeez, he shouldn't have done that!"

"He asked that you call . . . whoever, and tell them it wasn't his fault."

"He said that? Wow!"

They stared at each other. The smile stayed, but there was a sharpness in Manny's eyes. "Look, I'd like to help," he said, nodding, as though convincing himself that was his true desire, "but there's nothin' . . ."

"Richie said Manny could clear it up by speaking to some people who apparently are holding him."

Manny's eyes went flat. "Hey, I don't think . . ."

"Richie's family and friends are ready to go to the police. They know about your . . . umm, Manny's business with Richie. I don't know what that will mean."

"What the fuck you talking about?" No more smile.

Ralph said nothing.

Manny took a very deep breath. His eyes became slits. "Nobody goes to the motherfuckin' cops, or Richie is really gonna get hurt. Got it? You better make sure everyone knows that."

They glared at one another.

"Give me your phone number," said the guy Ralph was sure was Manny. "I'll make a call to New York and find out what's happening, then I'll give you a call. But don't make no fuckin threats, you got it?"

Ralph wrote his cell number on a pad from the glove compartment. He gave it to Manny. Manny slipped the paper into his shirt pocket. He turned and walked away.

Ralph drove off.

SEVEN

Manny El Bronx opened the garage door with the remote, slipped his black Lexus SC 400 inside. Just a couple of months old and driving like a beautiful bitch, she made him feel like a sporty business executive. He'd even started dressing better, picking up new shirts and slacks at Clubman.

He unlocked the iron-grated door, then unlocked the front door behind it. The first thing he heard was the kid crying. Manolito was in his playpen in the back room and he was wailing. Manny picked the kid up, took him into the living room and bounced him around. The kid kept on crying. Where the fuck was Josefina?

"Josefina!"

"*Si, si.*" She was out in the back, hanging up some clothes.

"The goddamn kid's crying! Get in here!"

"*Voy, voy. En seguida*, right away," said the old lady, who wasn't really that old—in her early fifties—but with a lined puss and a practically toothless mouth, the old bitch looked very old.

"The kid's wet," Manny said. "He's crying."

She came into the room with a big toothless smile, all four-foot-ten and eighty-five pounds of her. She put her short, surprisingly sturdy-looking arms out to Manolito. "What is it, little baby?"

"He's wet," Manny El Bronx repeated, then decided that he would change his year-old son himself. He laid the kid on the couch. "Bring me a Pamper," he told the woman who he paid more than enough to take care of Manolito while he took care of business around the city.

He changed the kid, then rolled a black-and-white soccer ball back and forth with him. Manolito started laughing. He tried to stand up, fell back down on his ass and laughed some more. Juanita said she would cook dinner and went to the kitchen.

Manny's cell phone rang.

"Yeah?"

"They want to talk to you."

"Yeah?"

"You better get your ass over there, in the back room of the restaurant in Isla Verde. They're pissed."

"Fuck 'em."

"At nine tonight. Just get your ass over there, or . . . it's your ass, you know what I'm sayin'? I'm just deliverin' the message."

"Later."

The kid started crying again; he wanted to play some more. Manny picked him up, carried him back to his room and dropped him in his playpen. The kid was really wailing now.

Shit!

He was hoping to get some sleep before he had to go out to Llorens again tonight. What time was it? Six-thirty by his diamond-studded Rolex, given to him by that asshole jeweler who couldn't meet his bill for the month's supply of *perico.*

He went into the kitchen. "Hey, go take care of Manolito," he told Josefina. "Don't worry about the food. I'll catch a bite later somewheres."

He went into his bedroom and lay down, burying his head in the pillow. The kid was still crying. He was about to shout out for Josefina again when the kid quieted down.

The louvers of the Miami windows were half open and the room was in creepy grayness. He stared up at the ceiling fan swirling slowly, his eyes following one blade around, wanting it to hypnotize him into sleep.

What the fuck did they want with him now? He had to at least make out he was listening. They were his suppliers. Good connections, he didn't want to fuck it up with them.

Was it because of the thing with that mule at the University? He had to do it. The kid made some good runs. They both prospered. So what if he'd screwed the kid this time around? He needed cash, quick. The kid swallowed, and most likely, shit out the 90 balloons with no problem, like before. So what if he told Papo that the Richie mule was packing 100 pellets. He needed the ten others he'd be getting pronto. He needed the $10,000 or so he was going to get for them to make the payoff to those fuckin' drug squad assholes. He'd already paid off *los dominicanos* for their cooperation.

Papo would blame Richie, which the professor guy said last night was happening. They'd keep the $5,000 the kid was supposed to get for the trip and make him withdraw more cash from previous trips. If he still had the cash. Which he'd better. If he didn't—well, who knew what that crazy fuckin' Papo would do?

Papo knew how to take care of business, he had direct connections to the South, with mules bringing up the *perico* and the shit from all over—Colombia, Mexico, PR, Santo Domingo, Argentina, Bolivia. Papo was a little crazy though. He knew of at least a couple of guys Papo wasted when they all were living in the Bronx. It had nothing to do with business though. Papo learned that the guys had touched his sister. He faced them down and they laughed about it so he blew them away.

Did they find out about the New York deal? The only one who was really getting fucked was the kid. O.K., he was sorry, but it was either Richie the mule or Manny. And it was no longer going to be Manny. He wasn't getting fucked anymore, like in the old days. He would be as nice a guy as he could be. Which wasn't always. Well, fuck it!

He could swear he still smelled her on the pillow, a tangy sweet smell, and some nicotine. He got a pain, in the heart.

Eight months ago. Fuckin ambulance came too late. Said they couldn't find the house. Dumb fuckers! Just when things were starting to go good, after all those shit, junkie-filled years. New house. Baby. Money starting to roll in. They were both quitting. Except for that night. He came home from a late night drop. Big score. He wanted to make love. To get inside her and stay in there, even after. Couldn't wake her, she had OD'd. Bastards came too late. On the way to the hospital, her eyes shot open. He never saw anyone so scared. Then she died.

They wheeled her into the hospital real fast like she wasn't dead.

He was off the junk, for good now. He had a kid to take care of. He had to make money, get a good life for his kid. He was just into it now as a business. He had his guys in lots of *puntos* around town. He took care of them. He was going to be a great Dad, a great boss! Take care of his own.

Fuckin' Angie. She couldn't make it. She was too weak.

Bite your fuckin' tongue. You asshole! You loved her!

He cried a little, then fell asleep.

Isla Verde Avenue was packed with cars creeping along, even in the middle of the week. Tourists and regulars were out for a night at the hotels, casinos, restaurants, and bars. He was forty minutes late for the meeting. Tough shit.

His Lexus crept down the avenue. Everyone—tourists, locals—dressing the same now, baggy fuckin shorts and sneakers. Except for the island babes. They still knew how to show their stuff. Sweet little dresses, designer jeans, heels four inches and higher. *Las locas,* the crazies, the boy-girls knew how to dress too. Hard to tell them apart from the real hookers.

He reached the restaurant, which was a Cuban place, a little further down from El San Juan Hotel. He pulled up in front and gave his keys to the valet-parking guy there.

Be careful, asshole. Don't gun the fuckin' motor!

He was hit right away with the meaty garlic smells of the Cuban restaurant. He told the guy who came up to seat him that he was looking for the meeting in the back room.

"Cómo no," said the waiter, in a black jacket and bowtie, leading Manny through the hubbub of the big main dining room to a much smaller room off to the side where one big table was occupied by three guys.

Manny said he was sorry he was late, too much fuckin' traffic. The one with the bushy black mustache told him to sit. The others grunted. All three were chomping away at steaks buried under fried onions and gravy.

Manny ordered a Don Q and 7-Up, and fried chicken with *Moros y Cristianos.* Only the fuckin asshole *blanquito Cubanos* would come up with that name for black beans and white rice.

He looked at the guys, waiting. Their eyes were on their plates like he wasn't there. One of them looked like a movie star on serious junk. He had black wavy hair and a long, handsome face, but his skin was a sickly pale and he wore large sunglasses. He kept sniffing. Another had no hair on his head or face and a barrel chest and a red and veiny face. He wore a pale blue guayabera with colorful flowers embroidered down the front.

The one with the mustache said: "When the fuck are you going to make good to those who help us carry out our business?"

So it had nothing to do with the mule in New York, which made Manny feel a lot better. The three jackass suppliers who, of course, worked for whoever the hell was above them, wanted to know why he had not "taken care" of the drug squad assholes. The bushy mustache noted that the "protectors" were trying to negotiate peace between some of the gangs so that everyone made out.

"These people have got to be paid, pronto! They got needs too," said Mustache, who was dressed in a blue blazer and white shirt opened three buttons down and who called himself "James Bond."

Manny was sure that 007 wouldn't have been caught dead, or alive, with that ugly hairy bug under his nose.

"The payments," Manny said, "are on their way."

"You got three more days to make them, or your supplies get cut," said James Bond.

"Definitely not a problem," said Manny. He finished his drink, ordered another, smiled at the poker faces around the table. He would make the payoffs as soon as his guys sold the *perico* he had kept from the mule. It would happen soon.

Manny ate, drank, paid for his meal, then excused himself to go to work. Bond shook his hand, the other two still made believe he wasn't there.

He drove back down Isla Verde Avenue, past the high-rise condos and the classy-looking houses near the beach. Eventually, he wanted to move with his kid to a house by the beach. Spend his time off running through the waves with Manolito. Where he lived now was O.K., call it middle-class with working people. It sure as shit was better than the projects, where he was raised, from the Bronx to Llorens Torres.

He wanted to move up again—soon.

What about that professor guy last night from the University? Fuck 'im. If he bugged him again, he'd say that Richie took off for Europe, or Mexico or South America. Go find him, asshole.

EIGHT

I really didn't plan it this way. But serendipity seemed, at first anyway, to lead me on.

The rest stop on the Jersey Turnpike happened to be not too far from Rutgers University. The rain soon stopped and I got more easily through the woods to some warehouses, homes, an open field, and a bunch of highways, including one going to New Brunswick and Rutgers.

I tried to thumb it; no one picked me up; I hiked along the highway. I finally reached a strip of pavement that took me into the town. I dried out walking under the afternoon sun. I would look for my cousin, Joey González, a student at Rutgers. Maybe he'd be able to lend me the money for a plane ticket back to Puerto Rico. Or I could make phone calls to arrange for the airfare.

Those guys were here, I wanted to be in Puerto Rico. They probably could catch up with me there. In fact, they could probably do it quicker than if I stayed in the states. But at least I'd be home. Sort of. Being a Nuyorican means you're sometimes confused where home actually is. I've spent the first eight years and the last two and a half years of my life in Puerto Rico; but, in the almost ten years between, I was truly branded by the Bronx. Still, just then my heart was hooked into Borinquen, what the Tainos called the island before the Spaniards came around and wiped them out. My heart had opened to Laura, my eyes to the beauty of the island where I was born, my mind to its place in the world.

Joey González was a second or third or fourth cousin, being my Mom's brother's second wife's son from her first marriage. I met him when he came on a vacation to Puerto Rico with his parents. About my age, he said he would be starting at Rutgers, going into pre-law. He said he was going to become an oil company lawyer and earn the big bucks. He told me he was selling pot back in Jersey and boasted he had bought a "slightly used" Porsche, which he hid from his "uptight" parents.

The truth is we didn't hit it off too well. He wanted Puerto Rico to become a U.S. state, which is O.K. because almost all Puerto Rican families are divided on the island's political future. But this guy was pretty damn self-righteous about it. America was the greatest, the best, the biggest—Puerto Rico was nothing, except for its Major League ballplayers. One day on the beach in Condado, we were arguing politics, then started pushing each other around, joking at first, then we got into a real fist fight. He gave me a black eye and I bloodied his nose. My uncle Pepe had to break it up. So we weren't on the best of terms.

But we were family. I hoped Joey saw it that way.

Pre-law is not really a major, which I learned after going around to several of the administrative buildings along College Avenue. I told the truth, up to a point. I was from Puerto Rico and I was looking for my cousin, there was a family emergency. I'm sure I looked dirty and ragged in my muddy and sweaty tee shirt and khakis, like I was the one with the emergency. But I was treated politely—maybe a little too politely, like they thought I might fly off the handle at any minute. I found that two José Gonzálezes were registered as students, and I actually was able to track them down.

The first José González was asleep when I knocked and knocked on the door of his dormitory room. I was about to leave when the door creaked open. This José-Joey was in his underwear and was small and skinny with a face like a peanut. He could barely keep his heavy-lidded eyes open. He looked drugged up. He wasn't my fat, six-foot cousin.

The next Joe Gonzalez was working in the library, where he was wheeling books around on a cart and putting them back in the stacks. When I told him I was looking for my cousin, who had the same name he did, he looked at me over nose-tipped glasses, shook his head and frowned, as though I was on some dumb, fruitless errand. "Well, I'm not him," he said like I didn't know.

So what I thought was serendipity wasn't turning out that way. Maybe Joey had dropped out of college and was working in Tío Pepe's restaurant in Union City, or he had transferred to another school. Or maybe he was and had been all the time, a student at Rutgers' Newark campus. Or maybe he was doing time in New Jersey State Prison for selling pot. Who the hell knew?

I kept seeing students who looked like Laura. My heart cramped at each "sighting."

It was getting dark and now my stomach was growling with hunger. I went to the campus cafeteria and waited for someone about to dump a half-filled tray, so I could ask for it. The guy I did ask laughed like I was joking. When he saw I wasn't, he bought me a Reuben sandwich and coffee and pie and told me to pay him back the next time I saw him.

If I ever see him again, I'll buy him a lobster dinner.

I walked around the town next, along the Raritan, past the frat houses, around the Puerto Rican slums—there seems to be at least one in every city in Jersey—by the bars and restaurants. I wound up late in the night on the grassy area fronting the Johnson & Johnson drug company building by the train station. I relaxed against the trunk of a tree. The next thing I knew a woman cop was shaking my shoulder.

"Wake up and get the hell back to your dormitory," she said not unkindly. She had big blue eyes and freckles across her nose. I watched her drive away, then crossed the street to the overpass under the train tracks. A couple of other guys were settled in there, sleeping on newspapers. One of them, an older man with dark brown patches on his light brown face, lent me a blanket. It was a mild night and the guy said he had a raincoat to cover himself with. He asked me where I was from. When I said Puerto Rico, his eyes got really large and he said: "What the fuck you doin' sleepin' on a filthy-ass street when you got all them beautiful beaches down there?"

I had no answer.

I fell asleep on a raised concrete slab until an early morning train overhead merged with the rumbling screech of the gigantic prehistoric something that was bearing down on Laura and me as we tried to outrun it across the University campus. It opened its huge mouth and we could see pouring up and out of its blood-red gullet Riot Squad cops swinging clubs and firing guns and missiles. Then I was ten years younger and I was asleep in my dream until someone started blowing smoke right up my nose and down my throat and I jump out of bed and see Mom rushing toward me, her hair looking electric, and we're both coughing like we're choking and tears are running from our eyes and the flames start licking out the windows and up the sides of our home.

As I shook myself awake, I felt nauseous but relieved also. There was an early morning chill and I put the blanket across the guy who'd lent it to me. He was snoring with a little smile on his face like he was sleeping peacefully in a bed at home.

I followed Albany Street to the Jersey Turnpike sign and stuck out my thumb. I was going to go back to the old neighborhood in the Bronx, the place where Mom and I lived for ten years after we'd left the island.

I was watching the sky go from gray to pink when a young guy in a black BMW swerved to a stop. He poked his blondish curly-haired head out the window.

"Where you headed?"

"New York."

"Whereabouts?"

"Anywhere."

"Cool. Get in."

I told him I was a visiting student from Puerto Rico and he said he worked on Wall Street and was into finance. He lived in Jersey and commuted daily to New York.

"I won't pay those fuckin rents there until I make my second million," he said, laughing.

We got onto the Turnpike. "Let's get some coffee before we take off for the city," he said.

We stopped at a service area that was a couple of miles up from the Joyce Kilmer, but I got nervous anyway. It was stupid, I know. Still, as we pulled in front of the building there, my legs got weak and my first thought was that Junior and Chucho were inside waiting for me.

The guy was out of the car and expected me to follow. So I did. No Junior or Chucho with switchblade opened, snarling by the door. I had to relieve myself like mad and wanted to wash my face, so I got brave and went into the bathroom. They weren't there either.

When I came out of the bathroom, the guy, his name was Graham, was holding two containers of coffee. He handed me a coffee and said, "Let's roll."

"How much do I owe you?" I went into my pants pocket, getting ready to fake an overnight loss of wallet and spare change.

"Forget it. You buy me lunch at the Windows of the World." He smiled at me. We both knew that he knew I was on the bum. I felt cruddy and stunk pretty bad and the bottom of my khakis and my sneakers were still caked with mud from my trek in the Jersey woods.

On the way, I told him that I had looked up a cousin who no longer was at Rutgers and I was now going to see friends in the Bronx before I returned to my home on the island.

He told me: "I got a secret for you. The business world sucks! I wish I could just rip off this suit and tie and take off across the country. See old girlfriends. Be a free soul. Like you."

I looked at his tanned face. He blinked long lashes, then winked a smiling brown eye at me. Was he pulling my string?

He put on a Paul Simon CD and we didn't say much more.

We got to New York in less than an hour. After coming out of the Holland Tunnel, he let me off at Canal Street.

"You got money to get up to the Bronx?" There was an amused smile on his face like he knew I didn't. Which pissed me off.

"Yeah. Thanks for the ride."

I walked down Canal Street, where sidewalk hawkers seemed to be pushing everything that was ever manufactured anywhere; then into Chinatown, where live and dead fish, all with staring eyes, were piled onto the outdoor stalls.

When I got up to the Bronx, my first stop would be Tony's apartment. He was my best friend from the very first day Mom and I moved into the building on Morris Avenue, he took me to the schoolyard and we played in a pickup game of softball. We kept in touch by email and last spring break from Hostos, where he's studying to become a gym teacher, he came down to the island for a week and stayed with me.

How to get up there? If I was caught hopping a subway turnstile—as we'd done in high school—this time around I could wind up in jail. So I decided to do what we once did as kids.

Tony, Pito and I were in the bleachers when Bernie Williams hit a homer to win the game—I almost caught the ball, it bounced two rows in front, then skipped just over my head. After, we decided to celebrate by walking from Yankee Stadium to a restaurant in Chinatown that Pito's uncle said was the best for the price in New York.

So, five or six years later, I took off by foot again, in the opposite direction. And again it was a fine walk. I rested for a while in Central Park, at both 59th and 110th streets. When I reached the end of the park, I even found a whole, edible apple inside a bag on a bench.

That was lunch, along with water from a public fountain. Then I went through El Barrio, down to First Avenue and across the Willis Avenue Bridge into the Bronx. I walked up to the Yankee Stadium just to see again the house built by Ruth with levels added by Gehrig, DiMaggio, Berra, Mantle, Mattingly—and Bernie Williams from Puerto Rico.

As soon as I hit the block on Morris Avenue and saw my old fire escape on the fifth floor, my legs got weak and my stomach tightened. Almost ten years, almost half my life, I lived in that building. Tony lived on the third floor, with his mom, two sisters, and a little brother. His old man, who had been a security guard in a bank, was shot trying to stop a holdup. It happened a couple of months before Mom and I returned to Puerto Rico. It shook the whole neighborhood, which everyone said was getting safer since the worst days in the 1970s and 1980s. It seems every time life gets better, something happens to make it worse. One step forward, then two steps back. Maybe that could be reversed in a long-enough life. I sure hope so.

The dark hallway smelled of the same antiseptic cleaner that Mr. Bonilla, the super, used to mop the floors with. I wondered if Mr. Bonilla was still super, living in the basement apartment with his wife and six kids, ages one to six. The elevator had that same antiseptic odor of the hallway mixed with the smell of all the dogs that lived in the five-story building. On the third floor, there were Puerto Rican cooking aromas: sizzling garlic and *adobo*.

I rang the bell to Tony's apartment. His mother opened the door.

I was shocked to see Mrs. Cotto. She was a short woman, just a little over five-foot-tall, but I remembered her as being put together very nicely, with a cute, bright face. Now, she seemed to have flattened out, looking even shorter and very heavy. The small features on her face seemed tiny and encased in fat, and her skin had gone from cinnamon color to a sort of yellowish brown. She wore a white sleeveless blouse and the flab under her arms was very noticeable.

But her smile hadn't changed. She still had wonderfully white, even teeth and her face lit up like the old days when she realized who I was.

"*Ay, mi'jo, cómo estás?* And your mother, how she is?"

I told her we were fine. I hoped she and Tony and her other kids were the same.

"*Bien, bien,*" she said. "Eva, she will graduate next week from high school. She is getting a scholarship for college."

"That's great!"

Puerto Ricans love to share good news right away. Then they reluctantly tell you the bad stuff, usually building up to anger or tears.

It's been more than two years since "*la tragedia*," she said, and the family was finally starting to get things together. Until . . .

"Now Pablito needs another operation on his little heart."

She continued: Little Pablo was born with a heart problem and he had one operation when he was a baby. The family got some money from the government, and St. Anthony's church had a benefit to help pay for the operation, but they still needed many thousands of dollars. So Tony is at his night job, which he just started last week. He also works during the day fixing cars at his uncle's garage in Queens, which he's been doing since he dropped out of Hostos.

"*Ay*, I'm so worried! He works from six p.m. to two in the morning—and what's the job? A security guard! And where? In a building on the Concourse. Three blocks down from . . . Oh, what's the use? I screamed and I cried about it enough. It's just for a few months, he swears to me. After the summer, he'll return to college. He swears to me he will."

Eva will get a job while she goes to college, her mother said. Then, when Pablito comes back from the hospital and gets better, and as soon as she could arrange for daycare for five-year-old Suzie and three-year-old Pablito, Mrs. Cotto will also look for something, maybe as a cook in a restaurant. Then Tony could return to school.

"*Así es la vida*," that's life, she said with a brave smile, only a small tear in a corner of her eye. After taking a very deep breath, Mrs. Cotto looked me in my eye, as though she saw something there that disturbed her. "Have you eaten?"

"Well, I . . ."

"Come in, please. We have *carne guisada*. Tony didn't eat, he had to work late at the garage, then he went to the other job, and Eva has started eating like a bird. So there's plenty."

Beef stew! With potatoes, green peppers, onions, olives stuffed with pimientos! There was no way I could say no.

I mopped up two plates with bread. Eva served me. She was no longer a kid and had turned out to be a real beauty: long, straight black hair, golden skin, dark brown eyes, curves in all the right places. On the inside of her left arm was a small tattoo that I couldn't quite make out. All I could think of to say between gulps of food was, "So where are you going to college?"

"Hunter." She intuited my next question: "To study languages? I want to be an interpreter. Maybe work for the United Nations?"

Her hopeful smile made my heart flip. Her eyes gleamed when she smiled. Like Laura. I wanted to hug and kiss her. All I could come up with was, "Great!"

I thanked Mrs. Cotto profusely for the dinner, and Eva and I, not being able to think of anything clever or heartfelt to say to one another, exchanged long smiles, and then I went to visit Tony.

The Babe, Mickey Mantle, Roger Maris and lots of other Yankees once lived in the building where Tony worked. Now a city-run apartment house for the elderly, it was once the Concourse Plaza Hotel. Like the rest of the Bronx, it fell apart in the 1960s and became a welfare hotel before it was renovated and turned into a place for the old folks. I knew of its rep from the Morris Avenue old-timers, especially from the few old Jews left in the neighborhood. Nat, the butcher, said he had his bar-mitzvah there and so did his son. His daughter was married there. The place had been "as classy as the Taj Mahal."

On my way over I decided I wasn't going to ask to borrow any money. Tony and his family had their own problems. Also, I wasn't going to ask Mom for the plane ticket money, even if it was only a loan. She had spent enough on me, helping with tuition, school books and rent—besides pushing me to keep studying for the master's degree I would need if I still wanted to teach at a university. I get grants and scholarships, but they don't cover everything. O.K., I had close to a four-point average when I graduated with my bachelor's in history and political science. Great. But I still have a long way to go, to learn and to understand. Learn what? Everything worth knowing.

I'd get to a phone and call Mike Padilla and get the money from him for the flight back. His parents were well-off and I knew he could easily get the money. When I returned to the island, I'd do what Tony had to do—drop out of school for a while and get a job. An honest one. I only needed nine more credits for my master's, which I could get at night while I was working.

When I rang a bell outside, Tony came around from a desk in a little office off the lobby to open the front door. There was a silver badge on his short-sleeved white shirt. He looked at me and did a double take.

"Jesus H. Christ! What the fuck you doin' here?"

"Visiting you, *hermano*."

We embraced.

"So what's up, bro?"

I told Tony everything. I got it all out and felt better, even though I realized more than ever what kind of hole I was in.

"Je-*sus*! You really fucked up, bro."

"Yeah, well I got fucked by that Manny *cabrón*. Right now I have to make arrangements to get back to Puerto Rico. It's not too late, maybe I could make a phone call now to the island."

Tony went back to the desk, handed me a cell phone.

My notebook with phone numbers was in the bag I had left in the car when I took off on the Turnpike. I didn't know Mike's cell number by heart, so I called information and got the number of Señora Súarez, the landlady who lived on the first floor.

After six or seven rings, she answered. She sounded groggy. It wasn't ten o'clock in the evening in Puerto Rico, but maybe she'd been sleeping. I could see her gray head bending on her scrawny neck and her rimless glasses sliding to the tip of her nose as she leaned to the receiver. I apologized and asked if she could see if Mike was in the apartment upstairs. She said she'd been in bed. I apologized again and again until she said she would go to the apartment the first thing in the morning, I should give her a phone number.

I quickly explained to Tony and he wrote down his cell number and I gave it to her. After several repeats, she read back the correct number and hung up.

"You sleep over my place tonight," Tony said.

We spent the next four hours talking about everything—old times, old friends, the shitty political situation in Puerto Rico, the Yankees, and so on.

When Tony got off at two a.m., we walked the six blocks back to 1059 Morris. I slept on a couch in the living room.

It was good to be sort-of home again.

NINE

There it was below—scrubby, scraggly, yellowed, pocked, cratered. Littered with discarded, rusted planes and tanks and trucks. There, below, the western part of the 21-mile-long island, was where, Tere knew, that for more than half a century, the Navy has been dropping bombs, exploding devices, strafing live ammo, shelling from ship to shore, experimenting with napalm, agent orange, depleted uranium, white phosphorous, arsenic, mercury, lead, cadmium and other killer chemicals. On the eastern end of the island, it was lushly green and unpopulated; the Navy stored its munitions there. Jumbled between were houses and roads and the thousands of residents. All around the island edges were those beaches that visitors found among the most beautiful anywhere. The white sand was lapped by sparkling turquoise waters. Tere also knew that tons of unexploded munitions lay in the waters and around some of the beaches. The plane zoomed low over horses and cattle chomping on grass. The pilot pointed out the bioluminescent Mosquito Bay that glowed at night.

The single-engine Cessna carrying Tere and a half dozen other passengers on the 20-minute flight from San Juan landed smoothly on the lone runway. Tere was greeted by Sara Muñiz, a hefty middle-aged woman in a red T-Shirt that said *"Ni Una Bomba Mas"* (Not One More Bomb), and jeans tucked into Army boots. She had a beauty mark low on her forehead that looked like the decoration worn by Indian women.

"Welcome to Vieques." They embraced.

Tere had met Sara several days before when Sara had come to San Juan to ask if Legal Services would represent families in a class action against the Navy. Tere came to the offshore island to sign up residents for the suit that would ask the court to order the war games moved someplace unoccupied by human beings. That was the main objective, along with getting the Navy to pay the mounting medical bills.

"There's a bunch of people who'd like to meet you. They'll be coming to the Peace and Justice Camp. They just set up the new camp last week after the Marines and the cops knocked down all the other settlements on the target range," Sara said, revving the motor of the old Jeep Wrangler.

She maneuvered the jeep up a hill, then onto a rutted road, then down an incline and onto another road, this one paved and smooth. She handled the vehicle like a pro.

Sara plunged right into the recent arrests that cleared the target zone of the protestors. "It was like World War III. They came in helicopters and they were armed to the teeth. It was unbelievable."

The jeep cut across a field and Sara beeped at several horses nearby eating grass and nuzzling each other.

"They arrested everyone. I was home taking care of the kids at my day-care center so I wasn't picked up. But they locked up nuns, for Christ's sake! For what? For protesting against the bombs and the shelling from the ships and the chemicals, poisoning the air and the water, making so many sick. It makes *me* sick that all this is happening in a U.S. territory. What does this say about our humanity, for Christ's sake?

"Have you always lived here, in Vieques?" Tere asked.

"No. My husband is retired Army. We lived all over the states and Europe before he retired and we came down here where he's originally from. To be honest, I don't give a damn about politics. All I know is what I see, which is lots of people and too many kids getting sick. Imagine if they were doing this in the states on an island where nine thousand people lived. They'd never get away with that!" She revved the motor again up another bumpy road.

They arrived at the Peace and Justice Camp. Several wood-and-corrugated houses were hammered together on a hillside under mango trees right across from the gated entrance to the Navy's Camp García and, further on, the target range. A couple dozen Riot Squad cops stood and sat around by the gate, looking bored as hell.

Tere met them all: the environmental and political activists, the politicians and fishermen and priests, nuns and ministers, the teachers, the housewives and mothers and dads and kids. She was given studies by doctors showing that the people living on Vieques had a 30 percent higher cancer rate than those who lived on the main island, as well as higher rates of diabetes, hypertension, heart disease, asthma, and other breathing problems and cirrhosis of the liver. The infant mortality rate was 25 percent higher. She was given the results of a study by Dr. Jorge Colón of the UPR, who found in hair samples he took last year that 34 percent of the residents had toxic levels of mercury, 55 percent had lead contamination, 69 percent were contaminated with arsenic and with cadmium, 90 percent with aluminum, 93 percent with antimony—all of which were found in the ordnance used during the Vieques maneuvers.

People lined up all day to sign up as plaintiffs in the suit against the Navy, the Secretary of the Navy, the U.S. government and the president of the United States. Tere listened patiently, taking notes: "No hospital on Vieques. The sick must take the ferry for treatment at hospitals on the main island. Emergencies? Are they helicoptered out? "

She wrote: "Aida Fernos, her 10-year-old twin daughters, Mily and Sylvia, diagnosed two years ago with stomach cancer. Both girls had intestines removed.

"Leonor de León, school teacher, almost all the 25 kids in her third-grade class, asthma and other breathing problems. The kids always coughing and spitting up. 'It's like a damn TB ward in my classroom.' Teacher, in her early 20's, coughing, herself."

Sara Muñiz told Tere her niece's story: "The doctors found all sorts of foreign chemicals in Ceci's blood and her family was sure the toxic metals released during the Navy's exercises had caused Ceci's cancer. She's had nine tumors cut out from her little body already, including from her brain, and a kidney, and her hand, and a leg, and a shoulder. My brother Carlos and sister-in-law Ana, they took Ceci to a hospital in Boston, where she's getting chemotherapy treatment. She's got no hair. Lots of time she's jumping around like any other four-year-old, but she's dying."

Sara's eyes teared up. So did Tere's.

Tere learned that the Navy was getting ready to start bombing and strafing and exploding mines again and that the people of Vieques would continue protesting. She wanted to get back to her office to write up the papers and file the suit immediately in federal court in San Juan.

Amidst all the misery, she also felt . . . exhilarated. Finally, she would be doing something worthwhile.

Tere Jiménez, a scholarship student and the family's first college graduate, finally would be returning to that which she had been educated for at the New York University Law School. She'd be returning with the added if the unrealistic principle that had been instilled into her psyche by one Professor Maria Lepre: "The practice of law should be defined by justice, not by territory, money, power or process."

After three years in the cherry-wood paneling offices of Maxwell and Rosen on Court Street 'in beautiful downtown Brooklyn , concentrating on power and process to further enrich the leaders of the corporate world, Tere finally understood that she'd rather be doing lots of other things, such as marrying, raising a daughter, and even running a Laundromat in Puerto Rico. *Mami*, and especially *Papi*, had conniptions.

Pete Jiménez didn't leave his homeland and drive a cab for so many years before starting a limo service with his two brothers so that his only daughter, who was so smart and so beautiful, who he helped pay her way through six long years of college, though he admitted she had paid back some when she started lawyering, he didn't raise that young lady so that she could wind up doing such a dumb thing as quitting a position, where she was heading for an unworried life, as far as financial security was concerned.

Sorry that I let you down, *Papi*. But at least I'm back truly . . . lawyering.

The law school grind, waitressing after classes and on weekends before joining that tony law firm, convincing herself she was on the right track until she realized she wasn't. Then, thanks to God, Ralph Camacho, and beautiful, precocious Diana. Ralph, more intelligent, more tenacious, more compassionate than he, himself, knew. She knew. He would make a living and a career as a writer and she would do what she could to help, even if it meant, for a time, piling into machines and folding up other people's smelly socks and stained undies.

When they moved to Puerto Rico—she had only been here on a couple of vacation visits—she realized that her true homeland was Flatbush, Brooklyn, New York. Ralph got it. In those first years, they flew up on lots of weekends to see her friends, her family.

Gradually, she settled in.

Former Corporate Lawyer Runs Laundromat—And Likes It! (up to a point)

O.K., she did the time. Now it was . . . well . . . her time. She would work long and hard for these people on this dot in the wide sea.

So, what are we here for, if not to try to right obvious wrongs, to help others?

That, thought Tere, was about as profound as she got.

TEN

It had been a warm night and I was in my underwear. I'm a light sleeper and when Tony's sister Eva crossed the room in the morning, I heard her give a little gasping chuckle. I looked up and saw two startled eyes looking down—at the bulge in my shorts. Vaguely remembering a dream in which she had a leading role, I reached for the cover that wasn't there. I turned on my stomach and buried my head in the pillow and faked sleep until she left for school.

Before going to work at his uncle's garage, Tony lent me his cell phone. He also gave me undershorts, socks, a blue button-down shirt and another pair of khakis to replace the funky clothes I had been wearing for days. I spent the next hours waiting for a call from Mike Padilla.

Mrs. Cotto had taken Pablito to a doctor's appointment and I was baby-sitting Suzie, who had spent half the night crying from a bellyache, and was napping in her room. I looked over Tony's books and decided to read *Misery* for about the tenth time. I was back lying down on the couch when Eva came home from school. She said hello shyly and snuck a glance down to my crotch, which was now covered by khakis. We both blushed. She was carrying a book.

"What are you reading?" I asked.

"Love in the Time of Cholera." She looked down at the cover of the book, as though to make sure of the title. "I'm rereading it because it's so beautiful. Have you read it?"

"No," I had to admit.

"It's about two old people who've been in love all their lives, but only were able to get together near the end." She turned to the last page in the book and read:

"The Captain looked at Fermina Daza and saw on her eye-lashes the first glimmer of wintry frost. Then he looked at Florentino Ariza, his invincible power, his intrepid love, and he was overwhelmed by the belated suspicion that it is life more than death that has no limits."

Eva blinked several times. "That's so beautiful."
I nodded.
"Would you like to borrow it?" She held the book out to me.
"I . . . umm . . . sure, but maybe after you read it again."
We smiled at each other for a long time. She retreated into her room.

Eva was a real sweetheart. I wanted to knock on the door to her room and invite myself in and . . . who knows what?

I still loved Laura, with my head and my heart. But there were other parts of my body . . . Forget it!

I went back to *Misery*. I was into the suspense and the horror, but something else in that book got to me. I liked the way, in a novel-within-the-novel, the writer was forced to write something he didn't want to write—another book about Misery Chastain, the Victorian-Age woman he made lots of money off by writing about in stupid romance novels—but he gets so caught up in the writing that he turns it into a real work of literature. The made-up Misery and the "real life" Annie Wilkes—the crazy woman who keeps the writer, Paul Sheldon, prisoner—blend into some sort of tough-ass woman goddess who forces the literary art out of Paul.

Mrs. Cotto came home about an hour later and Eva came out of her room and went into the kitchen with her mother. When Suzie woke up again crying and Pablito started crying also. I decided to go out for a walk.

Looking into the *Estrella de Borinquen*, I saw Don Felipe stacking Goya products on the shelves of his colmado, which is what he was doing the last time I saw him, almost three years ago, the day Mom and I moved back to Puerto Rico. Don Felipe, I believe, had a crush on my mom. He always insisted on personally delivering to our apartment the groceries she bought, and she always offered him a cup of coffee or a glass of *maví* that Don Felipe fermented in the colmado, then delivered free to us. They sat at the kitchen table and talked about old times back on the island, and before he left they smiled and gave each other *abrazos,* and that was it.

I walked a couple of blocks toward the Concourse, past Roberto Clemente Junior High on 164th Street. Its doors were still painted green. I learned English there—well, actually, I learned it in the street and from TV—and I played stickball, touch football, and basketball in the schoolyard and, in the eighth grade, I had my first crush, on Sandra Álvarez, and for the first time my tongue touched another tongue in another mouth.

It was at Bobby Torres' birthday party. Someone saw out a window upstairs the snow coming down like big pieces of confetti and sticking to the sidewalk and the hoods of cars and we came up from the basement for a snowball fight and Sandra and I went to the closet for our coats. I pulled her in there and shut the door and we fell among the parkas and raincoats and jackets and went at each other's mouths like we were resuscitating one another and our tongues tipped, then thrust and we continued deep kissing and tongue-touching. She tasted like the peanut butter crackers she had been eating. We stopped when someone knocked on the door to get a coat . . .

Nice memories. But now all I could think of was that that fuckin Mike Padilla hadn't called.

I sat on a curb and rang up *Señora Súarez* again. She told me that she had gone to Mike's apartment early in the morning, but he wasn't there.

"I left a note for him to call you at the phone number you gave me," she said. "He hasn't called?"

"No, not yet. I hate to bother you again, *señora,* but could you just see if he's in the apartment now? I'll wait."

There was a pause, an *"¡Ay, bendito!,"* then: "I will try once more."

"Gracias."

Several minutes later: "He is not there. The note also is not there."

"Could you . . .?"

The line went dead. Now fuckin what?

Then as I was returning to Tony's building, the cell phone he had lent me rang.

Mike, finally!

"Hey, motherfucker, we know where you are and we're gonna track you wherever, so if I was you I wouldn't run. You got one last chance. Show up at eight tonight in front of the hotel on Broadway where we was the last time. With the money you owe. If you're not there, you are so fucked. Because we'll come to get you, *cabrón.* You're gonna die!"

It was Chucho, the little asshole whose head I had cracked open. How did they find me? Or get Tony's cell phone number?

I didn't want to involve Tony and his family in any of this. I'd call him later and tell him why I had to take the cell phone, then I'd return the phone with box seat tickets to several Yankee games. Right then, I had to get the hell out of there.

ELEVEN

Ralph read his students' essays while waiting in the Laundromat for Doña Juana, who would run the place in the afternoon:

In due course they found themselves entering the narrowest part of the winding straits. Rugged cliffs hemmed them in on either side, and Argo, as she advanced, began to feel a swirling undercurrent. They moved ahead in fear, for now, the clash of the colliding Rocks and the thunder of surf on the shores fell ceaselessly on their ears . . . Once more the rocks met face to face with a resounding crash, flinging a great cloud of spray into the air. The sea gave a terrific roar and the broad sky rang again. Caverns underneath the crags bellowed as the sea came surging in. A great wave broke against the cliffs and the white foam swept high above them. Argo was spun around as the waves reached her . . . now another overhanging wave came rushing down on them, and when Argo had shot end-on like a rolling-pin through the hollow lap of the terrific sea, she found herself held back by the swirling tide just in the place where the Rocks met. To the right and left they shook and rumbled, but Argo could not budge.

This was the moment when Athene intervened. Holding on to the hard rock with her left hand, she pushed the ship through with the other; and Argo cleaved the air like a winged arrow . . . When the men had thus got through unhurt, Athene soared up to Olympus . . .

"The above description of Jason and the Argonauts sailing through 'the Rocks' and the intervention of the Goddess Athene reminds me of when my family, including my father, mother, little sister and two little brothers, were dispossessed from our home in Hoboken, New Jersey because my father lost his job at the factory and he refused to go on welfare and we couldn't pay the rent. I couldn't believe what I saw one day when I came home from school. Everything we owned in the world was on the sidewalk. I tried to get into the house, but the door was locked. Then I saw my mother and sister and brothers coming down the street. They were all crying. They couldn't find my father and they couldn't get into the house. An hour later my father showed up with three friends who also had lost their jobs at the factory and they broke the lock on the door and moved all our furniture back into the house. Soon after, we got a loan from an uncle in Puerto Rico and we left for the island."

Nellie Feliciano

Aeolus aimed his trident at the shell of the mountain, and drove it into the wall: the winds like an invading army surged to where he had made the opening and blasted out across the world with hurricane force . . . Suddenly clouds removed the sky and the daylight from the Trojans' sight. Inky darkness hovered over the water. The heavens resounded, and the horizon sparked with a myriad lightning flash: everything seemed to the crews to threaten instant extinction . . . a mountain of water towered above them like a cliff. One ship, which carried the Lycians and stalwart Orontes, was swamped before the leader's eyes by a massive sea that crushed its stern: its helmsman was thrown clean off head first; but as for the boat itself, three times the wave spun it around violently on the same spot, before the churning whirlpool sucked it down into the deep. Aw could be seen swimming on the surging tide, amid weapons and wreckage and Troy's treasure.

Aeneas' limbs grew stiff with cold: he groaned, and extending both arms towards the sky he voiced such thoughts as these: "How blest indeed were those who had the good fortune to fall in front of their parents, before the walls of Troy! Diomedes, strongest of the Greeks, could you not have slain me, and released this soul of mine with your right hand on the plains of Ilium, where brave Hector lies, thanks to Achilles' spear, and mighty Sarpedon too, where the river Simois washes over so many shields and helmets sucked beneath its waters and so many corpses!" As he cried out these words, a rasping head-on blast from Aquilo smacked Aeneas' sail, and a wave lifted the ship skywards.

Neptune felt the sea moving and grumbling mightily . . . He was greatly displeased and calmly lifted his head above the wave crests, looking out far over the deep. He saw Aeneas' fleet strewn across the entire ocean, the Trojans swamped by the waves as destruction rained from the sky. "Do you dare, winds, without my authority, to throw land and sea into confusion, and to destroy such mighty achievements?" He sedated the heaving waters, gathered the clouds and dispersed them, and restored the sun . . .

Just as happens when a riot breaks out in a great city, and the ignorant crowd goes wild; now firebrands and stones begin to fly, and insanity fuels the fight; but then, if it happens that they see a man they look up to and respect for his achievements, a hush descends, they patiently lend him their ears. When he speaks, he wins control, and brings peace to their hearts and minds . . .

"Like Aeneas, who wished he was in Troy when the storm began to hit, I wished I had stayed at home in Puerto Rico that winter on Brook Avenue in the Bronx when the heat and hot water kept going off and a window got stuck at the top and we couldn't completely close it, and even the rats looked like they were shivering. We spent much more time than usual in the kitchen near the gas stove that was lit on all four burners. My *abuela*, Filomena, who lived with us, wound up in Lincoln Hospital with pneumonia and then we had to put her into the Morris Park Nursing Home, where grandma died soon after. Then Fred Johnson, who was a retired schoolteacher living on the ground floor, organized a rent strike. No heat, no rent, we told the super, who told the landlord, who threatened to take us to court.

"Then, in the middle of the night, there was a fire in the basement. My Dad was coming home late from someplace and smelled the smoke and woke all of us up, me, Mom and my two sisters, and we ran down the four flights and stood freezing outside while the fire engines drove up and the firemen put out the fire. Luckily, the fire was put out before it spread all over the building, but Fred Johnson's ground floor neighbor died of smoke inhalation and Mr. Johnson was brought to the hospital.

"He got out of the hospital the next day and we had a meeting in our apartment. Some of the tenants wanted to burn the landlord's home to the ground in revenge, but Fred Johnson, who had been in civil rights in the sixties, told us to keep our calm and continue the rent strike. He called the newspapers and there was a story about the fire and the strike and, eventually, the city took over the building and we got our heat and hot water back, at least until the next winter."

Jimmy Betancourt

"There were eight hundred people in that ship . . . Eight hundred living people and they were yelling after the one dead man to come down and be saved. "Jump, George! Jump! Oh, jump!"

I stood by with my hand on the davit. I was very quiet. It had come over pitch dark. You could see neither sky nor sea. I heard the boats alongside go bump, bump, and not another sound down there for a while, but the ship under me was full of talking noises. Suddenly, the skipper howled: "Mein Gott! The squall! The squall! Shove off!" With the first hiss of rain and the first gust of wind, they screamed: "Jump, George! We'll catch you! Jump!"

The ship began a slow plunge; the rain swept over her like a broken sea; my cap flew off my head; my breath was driven back into my throat. I heard as if I had been at the top of a tower another wild screech, "Geo-o-o-orge! Oh, jump!" She was going down, down, head first under me . . .

"I had jumped . . ." He checked himself, averted his face . . . "It seems," he added.

"Although I chose a scene where a 'storm' is less than physically ferocious, what happened that night on the ocean aboard the Patna certainly caused havoc in the life of Jim of Conrad's *Lord Jim.* He abandoned ship with the rest of the officers as they feared the damaged ship would sink. It was the one cowardly act in the life of Jim, who before that thought that he would live a life doing heroic things. When I read the scene, it reminded me of a day in high school.

"It was the first week of my first year at Dickinson High School in Jersey City. Classes were over for the day and I was walking across the yard to get a bus back home. It was snowing out and there was a big snowball fight going on. At least, that's how I was told it started before the blood began mixing in with the snow. Instead of snowballs, fists were flying between some Hispanic kids against twice as many black and white kids. The Hispanic kids were getting beat up. As I tried to scoot away to the bus stop in front of the luncheonette across the street from the school, a punky Irish-looking kid came running up and grabbed my coat. He announced: "Hey, here's another Spic."

"Two other guys took me by the arms and started swatting me in the head. I told them: "I ain't no goddamn Spic!" I spoke perfect English since we moved to Jersey City when I was six months old. "My parents are from Croatia," I said, which confused everyone.

"Then they brought a small and really skinny Dominican kid over to me. He was shaking. "Hit him!" they said. I slapped the kid hard across the face and his eyes teared up. "Punch him!" they said. I punched him in the mouth and he bled and the blood dripped into the snow. They let me go and I ran to the bus stop.

"Like Lord Jim, I'll never forgive myself for that."

Federico "Freddie" Del Valle

Towards evening of that day, the Pequod was torn of her canvas, and bare-poled was left to fight a Typhoon which had struck her directly ahead. When darkness came on, sky and sea roared and split with the thunder, and blazed with the lightning, that showed the disabled masts fluttering here and there with the rags which the first fury of the tempest had left for its after sport . . . All the yardarms were tipped with a pallid fire; and touched at each tri pointed lightning-rod-end with three tapering white flames, each of the three tall masts was silently burning in that sulfurous air like three gigantic wax tapers before an altar . . .

"Aye, aye, men!" cried Ahab. "Look up at it; mark it well; the white flame but lights the way to the White Whale! Hand me those main-mast links there; I would fain feel this pulse, and let mine beat against it; blood against fire! So."

"Only a madman like Captain Ahab in *Moby Dick* would see the flame-like charges on the tips of the masts caused by the electrical storm, which are known as St. Elmo's fire, as a sign that the typhoon-tossed ship is being led to Ahab's monomaniacal goal of killing the Great White Moby Dick Whale. In some way, this reminds me of what happened to Carlos Cruz, our next door neighbor in Brooklyn. I was eleven at the time and Carlos was thirteen. We played together and kidded around. I liked Carlos a lot, he had a great sense of humor, and once in the movies, he put his arm around me. But that was all. We never got really romantic. But there was one thing tragic. Carlos, at thirteen, was shooting up heroin, which he got from a cousin, Felipe, who was eighteen. And one day Carlos got very sick and admitted to his mother, who he lived with alone, that he was taking drugs.

"Mrs. Cruz, who was a very religious woman, brought Carlos to *Hermano* Jaime, who preached in a storefront two blocks down from our apartment house. *Hermano* Jaime told the people who came to his church that when he was living in Hoboken, N.J., a miracle happened in his life. He said that two heavenly beings took him to a marble hall where an apparition merged with his body and began to speak inside of him. He said that he became both Jesus Christ and Christ's brother, James. A voice inside him told him to move to Brooklyn and start up the *Trabajando Por Gracia* (Working for Grace) church. His followers wore T-shirts with *Hermano* Jaime's face and the slogan, "GOD HAS ARRIVED."

Hermano Jaime told Mrs. Cruz that the sickness was a sign from the Devil that he was inside the body of Carlos and would stay there and make Carlos do evil things. Carlos should come to the store-church every night so they could work to get the Devil out.

"Carlos went there every night for a couple of weeks and kept hearing about the Devil inside him. When I saw him one day he told me to stay away from him until he was "cured." He wasn't smiling. Then I found out he stopped going to see *Hermano* Jaime and instead of getting the Devil out, he again started feeding him, it, whatever, with heroin.

"Then Carlos decided there was only one way to get rid of the Devil. He did this by standing on a trunk in our apartment house basement, where many people stored their big luggage. He threw a jump rope around a fat pipe coming down from the ceiling and tied a loop in the rope. He put the rope around his neck and kicked away the trunk. He was thirteen years and nine months old.

"I'm not sure who stands for what in the book and in real life, but this is what came to my mind after reading the chapter called 'The Candles' in *Moby Dick*."

Migdalia "Miggy" Miranda

He had some terrific students this semester.

The semester before, in an assignment to compare the storm scene in *The Odyssey* to an event in their own lives, most of the students mentioned hurricanes on the island or snowstorms in the states that they had been through. Richie Pérez wrote that the scene when Ulysses was pitched into the sea and left adrift for nine days reminded him of when he and his mother were living for days in the basement of a Bronx apartment house. They'd sought refuge in New York after his drunken father set fire to their house. Richie, who was all of eight at the time, fought off rats for several days and nights in that dark, dank, freezing basement before he and his Mom found a home.

Well, like Richie, the other students now were catching on, comparing literary storms to upheavals in their own lives. Like Richie, they were beginning to understand the connective tissue between great literature and their own lives.

But where was the connective tissue that would lead to the whereabouts of Richie Pérez?

Would Ralph's visit to Manny El Bronx ease the latest tempest in Richie's life? Probably not. He should have pushed that sonovabitch harder, come up with a better threat.

He's got to help the kid. For Richie's sake, for Richie's mother's sake and, he realized, for the sake of Ralph Camacho. Something to do with Grandpa Max and Juan turning into Juanito the bum, as well as Richie's sonovabitch of a father.

Errant fathers, seeking sons.

TWELVE

"O.K., listen up. I want that asshole's money what's owed us, or I want the 100 grams of *perico*, or I want him cut to pieces with a machete, one body part at a time, with a ribbon tied around it. You understand what I'm telling you?"

"Yeah, sure, Papo. Jeez, I thought this kid was *vertical*, a standup guy, you know? First, he fucks me with the *perico*, then he screws you guys by taking off. I want to tell you how really sorry I am. You know, I'm your man. Ever since when I told the cops that you was with me when you done what to those *cabrones* who messed with your sister."

"Hey, listen up! I don't give a fuck what happened five minutes ago. You got paid plenty for the favor and we made a deal when you went back to the island."

"I didn't get paid every . . ."

"Here's something else. If I don't get satisfaction from that asshole I'm gonna make you feel it too, and I'll get another guy to deal for me in the Caribbean. I want you to see if he's back on the island and you let me know if you find that fuckin thief, I want that kid's money or his heart cut out and delivered to me, personally. You got it?"

"O.K., O.K., don't worry, *jefe*. We gonna . . ."

"*I* ain't the one who's got to worry. My boys are looking around here. If you find him first they gonna be sent down there to work wit' you. Get on this, like yesterday. I want to hear back from you, one way or the other. Don't have me call you again."

"Yeah, sure, Papo. I'm gonna . . ."

Dead phone. Dial tone.

So, Richie, the fuckin mule got away from them. So I'm gonna wind up getting screwed by that fuckin kid. Bullshit! I'm not gonna let this punk mule screw up my plans for the future. No fuckin way!

Manny El Bronx put the cell phone on the table next to his bed, picked up his watch. Nine in the fuckin morning! He only got to bed a few hours ago. Now the kid was crying. The damn kid was always crying lately. "Josefina!"

"Si?"

"Take care of the kid. Stop his goddamn cryin'."

"Sí, Señor."

He immediately felt guilty, and still in his undershorts went to the kitchen. Manolito was in his high chair, refusing to eat the oatmeal Josefina was trying to feed him.

"Gimme the spoon."

He made believe the spoon was an airplane coming in for a landing. The kid kept on crying. Manny El Bronx made louder airplane sounds, brought the spoon to his son's mouth and zipped it away. The kid got curious. Then he started giggling and eating.

"You got to make it like a game."

Like Angie did. A sad something tapped in his chest. He went back to his room. He could use another couple hours of sleep.

He flopped on the bed. He had to get Papo off his back. He had one lead for reaching Richie, that asshole professor who came to see him at Llorens. The kid must have gotten in touch with him. The professor had given Manny his phone number. What the fuck did he do with the paper?

His black silk shirt. He put the paper with the phone number in the shirt pocket. He got out of bed and went to his closet. A couple of dozen shirts lined up neatly. But the black one wasn't there. Shit!

Now he remembered. It was in a bundle with some other stuff for Josefina to put in the cleaners. Did he take the paper out of the pocket before he gave the shirt to Josefina? He looked in the night table drawer where he would have put stuff like that, then in the other drawers of other dressers and on the table where he kept miscellaneous shit. It wasn't there.

Fuck!

"Josefina!"

"Si, señor."

As he had told her, she put the clothes in the dry cleaners in the downtown shopping center, which she passed every day walking from the bus to her house.

"Did they find anything in the pocket of one of my shirts?"

"I don't know, *señor*."

"The ticket. Where's the ticket?"

"One moment. It is in my purse. The purse is in the kitchen."

She came back with the ticket. Manny called the phone number on it. The woman who answered couldn't help him. He asked to speak to the manager. The manager was having coffee in a shop next door.

"Go get him," Manny ordered. "This is very important."

"One moment."

No one came back on the line for several minutes. Then the line went dead. Manny cursed. He called again. He got a busy signal. He slammed the house phone down. He threw on a pair of pants, and a tee shirt and got into his loafers. Three fuckin hours sleep and he was off again.

He opened the garage door, got into his Lexus and took off for the shopping center. If he had to, he'd rip up the fuckin dry cleaners until he found that paper. Then he'd call that asshole professor, find out if he knew where that fuckin Richie mule was. Get Papo off his ass. Then get a couple hours more sleep.

THIRTEEN

The evening was coming on and I was wandering around, moving away from the old neighborhood, wondering how these guys got Tony's cell number and still waiting for Mike to call. I wound up down by Macombs Dam Park, across from the Stadium. The Yankees were on the road so there weren't crowds around. I passed by the baseball and the softball fields and the basketball courts, where kids were still playing despite the quickly waning light. When you're sixteen you keep playing until the ball becomes a pill.

Tony and I spent a lot of time on those fields. That was when I was hoping against hope to become the next Bernie Williams. I wasn't all that bad either. I made the team in my junior year at Morris High. I was a rangy center fielder and I had a good arm and wasn't a bad hitter. But, like so many Mantle and Mays wannabes, I had a real hard time hitting a good curveball. Anyway, now I play or used to play center field for a team in a softball league on the island.

The eight p.m. deadline to meet Junior and Chucho in front of the hotel on Broadway was about ten minutes away. Fuck 'em.

Goddamn Mike Padilla! He still hadn't called.

I walked down to a little park on Woodycrest Avenue, near the Major Deegan Express, and looked across the Macombs Dam Bridge. On the other side of the Harlem River, in Manhattan, was Coogan's Bluff. A housing project stood on what was once the Polo Grounds, where the great Willie Mays patrolled center field for the Giants. I was born too late to actually see him play. But what baseball fan never saw the film of The Catch? Willie made it in the World Series on the ball hit by Vic Wertz of the Detroit Tigers. Willie running with his back to home plate, his hat flying off, catching the ball over his shoulder on the warning track, more than 400 feet from the plate, twisting around, throwing the ball to the infield, falling to his knees.

I missed Mays and I missed seeing the great Roberto Clemente, though I went to a public school named after him.

I sat on a bench in the little park, tapping Tony's cell phone in my pants pocket, thinking of calling that asshole Mike Padilla again. I took out the cellphone. Guess what? It needed to be charged, which I had no way of doing.

It was starting to drizzle, and I was the only one on the benches. Some shaggy-haired guy walking his shaggy dog disappeared up Woodycrest. It got chilly and windy and the drizzle turned to a downpour. I hurried up the steps, passed Yankee Stadium, got under the elevated train tracks above River Avenue. Cars were blowing their horns in the street where I was walking, so I had to get back on the sidewalk. The rain was coming down sideways. I decided to keep walking to get out of the neighborhood so I didn't run into Tony and Eva. You never could tell. They would ask me what I was doing, and I would have to explain, and I wanted to keep them out of whatever the hell I was getting deeper into.

I got to Mount Eden Avenue. Across from the entrance to the train station, I saw in a luncheonette window a cardboard sign that read: "Dishwasher Wanted." I went inside and asked a big black guy behind the cash register if I could see the manager. The guy, who had gray wiry strands in his beard and a full head of kinky hair, said he was the manager. He had a French accent. I told him I wanted to apply for the dishwasher's job. He said I could start at six the next morning.

That night, I slept for a couple of hours on newspapers under the steps leading to the el trains. It was cold and it was wet, but I didn't mind. I had a job!

I got to the restaurant at grisly dawn and told the manager, Jean-Pierre, that I was broke. He nodded like he knew and made me three eggs and toast and coffee. He made me a thick ham-and-cheese sandwich for lunch. I had some left-over chicken fricassee for dinner. Jean-Pierre said he would take the food out of my salary— after I worked there a year. Then he broke into hysterics and slapped me on the back and gave me coffee and a piece of peach pie.

Jean-Pierre was at the cash register and seated people. Beside the kitchen cleanup, I bussed the tables. There were two waitresses for ten or so tables, one man behind the counter, and the cook and me.

The waitresses were Jean-Pierre's wife, Sylvie, a short woman with a perpetual smile on her round face, and Camille, his daughter, who stood tall and beautiful with deep, dark eyes and was the opposite of her mom in the smiles department. The counterman was Jean-Pierre's son, also named Jean-Pierre, who looked like a young Harry Belafonte. Mariano, the cook, was a *Boricua*, from the mountain town of Barranquitas. He had long sideburns that curved into his flabby cheeks. We all spoke to each other in a mixture of English, Creole, Spanish, French, and Spanglish. Work ended at nine p.m.— only 15 hours after I started. I was given a couple of hours off in the afternoon, which I spent napping on a tattered blanket and a pile of old aprons in a little storeroom behind the kitchen.

After work, Jean-Pierre said: *"À demain. Hasta mañana.* I see you in za morning."

I spent another night in outdoor sleeping. It was a cool, dry night and this time I slept on a bench in Claremont Park, making a pillow of a bunch of rags I found in a garbage can.

I felt like shit after waking from my fitful snoozes. Jean-Pierre fed me again and let me wash up in the storeroom, which had an old, rusty sink. Then I spent another fifteen hours of washing and scrubbing everything in sight in and around the restaurant, including Jean-Pierre's white Ford pickup and his ancient black Lincoln Town Car, both parked in a small alley between the restaurant and a couple of warehouses.

After work, I told Jean-Pierre I needed an advance, I was still broke.

He smiled and peeled off a crisp ten-dollar bill. Then he added one, then two singles. "Here is for the two days."

"O.K.?" he said. "No problem? *A demain?*"

He must have been paying me the Port-au-Prince minimum. I would've had to be working for him a couple of years to get the money together for a plane ticket back to Puerto Rico.

I thanked him and left the restaurant.

I walked up Jerome Avenue until I found a bodega where I bought a ten-dollar calling card for PR. I kept looking for a working public telephone. The first three I found had their receivers pulled off the hooks. I finally found one that worked; I knew who I wasn't going to call: that sonovabitch Mike Padilla.

I put in the code number and dialed long-distance information for Ralph Camacho's number in San Juan. Months ago, after one class when we were talking about traveling the world, I asked the prof whether he would mind if I called him occasionally during my "travels," which I had planned to make around Europe after I got my master's. He said to call him anytime, from anywhere. Well, he was my best bet.

"Professor Camacho? Hi, this is Richie Pérez, from your *Epics of the Sea* class."

There was a slight pause. Then Professor Camacho said: "Richie Pérez. I haven't seen you in class lately. Where have you been?"

"I been . . . off the island. For an emergency. Look, I got a problem, of which the most important part is that my ticket back to Puerto Rico was stolen, as was all my ID, my cell phone and just about everything. I have no money to buy another ticket, so I have to ask you for this great favor. I need money for airfare."

I'd pay him back as soon as I got to a bank in San Juan. I hated to do it, but I would have to go into my savings for the scholarship.

"What have you gotten yourself into?"

"Nothing, really. Just, well, they stole . . ."

"Who are they?"

"Just these guys."

"These guys," the prof repeated like he knew they were assholes and I was a dumbass for doing business with them.

There was a silence. I was considering whether to just hang up when the prof said, "I'll wire you the money in the morning at the main Western Union office on Broadway, just off Times Square. I've had money wired to me there when I lived in the states. Would three hundred dollars be enough?"

"That would be great! I'll be at the office first thing in the morning. *Mil gracias,* Professor Camacho."

He grunted.

I got on the subway at the Grand Concourse and 176th Street. I rode different trains all night. I didn't even have enough change in the morning for a cup of coffee. But Prof. Camacho came through with the wired cash just before noon. I immediately took the subway out to JFK. Now I could get some coffee and even a doughnut.

But another big problem. The guy behind the airline counter asked for ID. I told him I had lost my wallet with all my ID and my return ticket. He brought me into an office in the back. People there called their people in San Juan where I had bought the round-trip ticket. Then I had to phone the prof again. He told the airlines people that he would get a copy of my student ID from the University and send it to them by the computer. Then I wrote out a report for the police, saying I had lost my wallet somewhere in the city. The airline's people issued me another ticket, which I paid for, and I was cleared through security and was finally able to get on the close-to-midnight flight back to the island.

PART TWO

FOURTEEN

The first thing I did when I got back to the island was to go to my room for my ATM card to pay back Prof. Camacho. Then I took a bus into Old San Juan. I'd been to the prof's home twice before, at the beginning of each semester when he'd ask a bunch of students over for snacks and beer. Professor Camacho asked us about our lives. He and his wife seemed really interested in our stories, which, in truth, not that many professors seemed to care about.

It was the middle of the afternoon and no one was home so I decided to walk around. I was overjoyed to be back in Puerto Rico. I knew that Papo and his guys had connections down here, and they could still go after me, but you always felt safer on your home turf, which I realized no longer was the Bronx.

Still, everything felt heavy when I passed the statue of Ponce de Leon in Plaza San Jose, where Laura and I spent weekend evenings. The heaviness plunged deeper when I went down to the San Juan Gate beneath the Old City walls, where we had walked out to the end of the small, rickety wooden pier, and while it dipped down and slid up with the tide, we kissed forever under the dazzling stars. Then I went to El Morro Fortress, where you could see the bay bending into the never-ending sea; the sea that surrounds us, cuts us off from any other place, yet, for so many centuries, was our one and only link to the rest of the world.

Life in the Old City is lived between the ocean and the bay, whether it's the ribboned waves of the Atlantic sliding on the beach below the highest streets, or the calm waters that slap against the docks on the lowest streets. Almost anywhere you look, you see the water; it sets your bounds, but it can also stir your deepest feelings. That's what it does for me, anyway.

I had a couple of beers in Sam's Patio, then returned to Prof. Camacho's apartment, which was on the second floor of a restored two-story house. The prof was home.

"I'm glad to see you're back, in one piece," he said, giving me a tight *abrazo,* then looking at me with a strange happy-sad expression, like I was a long-lost something-or-other. "Get in here."

We went into the living room, which must also have been used as a study. One of the walls was lined with books and in a corner was a desk with a computer and printer. The professor said the photos and paintings on the walls were done by his 13-year-old daughter. I especially liked a painting of a small yellow dog trotting down the blue-cobbled streets in front of the San Juan Cathedral while the Cardinal, dressed in red, talked to a group of nuns on the cathedral steps.

The prof sat on a swivel chair by the desk and directed me to a Dominican rocker.

"What the hell were you doing up to in New York that you had to call me as though it were a matter of life and death?"

I smiled, sort of sheepishly, then dug into my khakis and took out the $300. I handed him the envelope with the bills and he put it on a table without looking inside.

"I don't know how to thank you, Professor Camacho. I was in a real bind up there."

He nodded and waited. And waited.

Then I gave him a stammering explanation, followed by a righteous justification, an angry declaration, and a heart-rending confession.

I gave him the whole story, in sequence, from the day Laura and I met to the day of the Vieques protest at the University and what happened. I confessed my guilt at convincing her to go to the demonstration, told how the funeral left a hollow space in my soul, about the idea for the scholarship and not being able to get the money—I went to the unions, and the banks, and the pharmaceutical companies that make millions down here paying almost nothing in taxes, and some people were sympathetic but no one came up with anything. So then I got this meeting with Manny El Bronx, arranged by a friend who had a four-point average but dropped out of the University after his Dad killed his Mom. I told the prof how I became a drug mule and how the three earlier trips went smoothly, $5,000 each trip. Then I told him about this last trip and the thing about the capsules and how Manny El Bronx screwed me and what happened after and now how I'm thinking about ways to get revenge on that fuckin Manny El Bronx.

The professor's index finger tapped at his lip. I could see a mixture of things in his eyes: impatience, wariness, possibly real sympathy, but also disdain—like he was trying to figure out if I was stupid or ignorant or naïve, or maybe all three, with some bravura thrown in.

"I know these guys have contacts down here," I said, "but I'm thinking that I'm going to resume my life like before. I'll come up with another way to get money for the first year's scholarship. But I will *definitely* get the scholarship started."

Prof. Camacho continued to say nothing. This time his eyes went over my head, to some books, which he squinted at, as though the titles would tell him what I should do, or what he should say next.

Then he said: "I don't think it's a good idea to make believe nothing has happened. You're dealing with people who feel they will be diminished if you stay in one piece while refusing to do what they tell you to do. I'd put things on hold for a while."

What was I supposed to do, continue on the run for the rest of my goddamn life? I didn't say anything, but the prof seemed to see my anger and frustration. When I got up, he looked surprised. "Where're you going? Let's see what other possibilities we can come up with."

So I sat again and we talked. And came up with—not too much. I definitely was not going to go to the "authorities." I wasn't going to give names and be locked up as a drug mule. And I sure as hell wasn't going to pay off those bastards with my savings from the earlier trips. I'm going to see that the scholarship goes through, no matter what.

The prof insisted that I lie low. How, where, for a how long? A key jangled in the apartment door. "Hey, I'm here." Professor Camacho's wife came into the room.

"You remember Steve Pérez?

"Sure. One of your favorite students." Mrs. Camacho had beautiful white teeth. She was dressed in a plain white blouse, a black skirt and heels, and black-rimmed glasses. She tossed a black leather briefcase on the yellow-and-green striped couch and plopped down in the middle of the sofa. She looked like the teacher every kid in middle school gets a crush on.

"I thought you were going to pick up Diana," the professor said.

"She's sleeping over at Melissa's. They have a math test tomorrow, so they're studying together—for at least ten minutes before they start with the cell phones, the CD's, the TV."

Then Mrs. Camacho asked me, "Would you like to stay for dinner?"

We both looked at the prof. He nodded.

"Gracias."

"Bueno, I'll shower while the cook here warms up the *arroz con pollo*, which he assured me he was cooking this morning while I was in court."

"It's all set to go," said her husband.

Mrs. Camacho reappeared, changed into jeans and a T-shirt that said in the front: "Navy Out of Vieques."

"The bottom of the shower curtain is still moldy," she told her husband.

"There are only so many hours in the day," said the prof. They laughed and she touched her husband's cheek.

After a great dinner, Professor Camacho asked me if he could explain my situation to his wife. I said, "Sure."

She listened, nodding with a serious look on her face, just like a lawyer hearing out a potential client. The prof said again that I should disappear for a time, while I repeated I wanted to pick up where I left off, at the University at least.

The lawyer kept nodding like everything was a good idea. But then I saw her give her husband a quick flashing look that meant, I'm sure, "What the hell have you gotten me into?"

She took a deep breath and looked down at her fingernails like she was deciding whether to paint them right then and there. Then she said that besides waiting for a decision on the suit to try to stop the bombing on Vieques, she was representing thirty-two of the women arrested in the recent demonstrations that had halted the Navy maneuvers. All the women refused to post bail when some of them couldn't raise the money. Several were schoolteachers who felt guilty because the Department of Education, it seemed, didn't have enough substitute teachers to take over their classes. There was Sister Margaret Quinn, who was running a school with two other nuns in Barrio Tamarindo, high up in the mountains in the center of the island, near the town of Jayuya. The other nuns had taken part in the Vieques demonstration and remained in jail, so Sister Margaret was having a hard time running the school by herself.

I nodded, wondering what this had to do with my predicament.

"The people living there are poor as church mice," Tere Camacho said. "Some still cook over open fires and there is almost no refrigeration. But they are anxious to keep the school going. The kids go to the school free and the parents do construction work and cooking and cleaning and they sew the school uniforms. They want their kids to continue learning. So they're looking for a couple of volunteer teachers for the rest of the term, about another month. The grades are first to third. How would you like to start your professorial career teaching in elementary school? You'll get free housing up there."

"Until when?" I asked.

"Until," said Professor Camacho, "You're out of danger and the nuns are out of jail."

"How and when will that happen?" I asked.

"Let us work something out," the prof said. "I won't arrange anything until I talk with you."

"I'll have to think about it," I said. "I'll let you know in the morning." I thanked them for the dinner and got ready to go.

"Where are you going now?" the prof asked.

"To my place. In Río Piedras."

He looked over to his wife. "Not the best idea. You could be tracked back there fairly easily. Spend the night here on the pullout couch, then we'll drive up to Barrio Tamarindo in the morning. You could look around then make the decision."

O.K. What the hell?

So here I am, in Barrio Tamarindo, in what is called an "isolated community," in the Cordillera Central mountain range, in the highest part of the island, in my new living quarters, a one-room wooden shack with a cot, a couple of wooden chairs, a table to work and eat on, a small stove, a plastic cooler for ice and food, a pocket-sized transistor radio and a black-and-white TV. Also, running water.

I agreed to give it a go. I took my computer and some books, clothes and a few other things from my Río Piedras apartment and left a note for Mike Padilla, who I hadn't seen since I came back, telling him I was moving "out on the island," without saying where.

I called my Mom to tell her I was back, but I couldn't make it to her house this weekend because of a project I had for school, I had to spend lots of time in the library. I told her not to worry, everything was fine.

"Where were you all this time?" she asked.

"I was in New York. I was visiting relatives of Laura. They wanted to talk to me about setting up a scholarship at the University in Laura's name. They wanted to meet me, in person, and they didn't want me to say anything about their plans. Not yet."

"You couldn't have told your mother?"

"Mom, I gave them my word."

"O.K., sonny boy, I don't deserve your trust."

I didn't say anything. Sometimes she can be very difficult.

"When am I going to see you?"

"Very soon, mom. I promise. I have a few things I have to take care of. They're really important."

"O.K.," she said. "Finish up what you have to do, then come out here as soon as you can."

"*Bendición*, mom. Give me a blessing."

"*Que Dios te bendiga.*"

After a while, she understands. And accepts. After a while.

Ralph and Tere—that's what the prof and his wife told me to call them—brought me up to Barrio Tamarindo Friday evening. They gave me a day to settle in, then came up again on Sunday when we met with Sister Margaret. She was a small, crusty old nun with piercing blue eyes. Originally from Brooklyn, she lived in Puerto Rico for the past thirty years. She walked with a cane, which she also used as a pointer when later she took me around to show me who lived where and who would do construction work or provide food or sew the kids' clothes, all gratis, for the tuition-free school that got private donations. When she smiled, her face softened like a little girl's. She always smiled when every few minutes her pupils ran up to hug and kiss her as we walked through the barrio.

Ralph drove us to a nearby hotel that was once a coffee plantation and we had a large lunch that included pork, rice, beans, *mofongo*, avocado salad, *flan*, the works. We talked about Vieques and the upcoming protestors' trial, and Sister Margaret talked about the students, many of whom were progressing in school as well or better than those from more well-off families, because, Sister Margaret said, "God didn't give out brains according to the money in people's pocketbooks."

We went back to the barrio and Sister Margaret said she would see me early Monday. While Ralph and Tere took the twisting mountain road back to San Juan, I returned to my new home. There was literally nothing on the TV, which didn't seem to be working. I picked up my spiral notebook and tore out a whole bunch of pages with class notes on them. Then I made the big decision: to start writing a journal about life and all the things I sure as shit don't know about it.

FIFTEEN

The manager of the dry cleaning store chomped on his cigar calmly. There was no need to panic. The slip of paper with the telephone number on it was in the cash register, waiting for retrieval.

"We would have given it to you when you picked up your stuff," said the manager. "See, we put the number of your ticket on the paper so when you come in . . ."

Ash from his cigar fell among the coins in the register.

"Yeah, whatever," said Manny. "Thanks."

"Hey, professor, you got to excuse me for not getting back to you earlier, but a couple of things had to be worked out for the mule. So let me just say, they been *almost* worked out, I just need to get some information on a couple of more things. I know the kid is back in PR, I heard about it, people tell people, I got to contact him soonest. Maybe you know where he is? He's got to be contacted for things to get cleared up."

He took the chance like he knew where the mule was at. A long pause on the line. "Hey, you still there?" asked Manny El Bronx.

Finally: "I'll get word to Richie. Tell me what he has to do."

"That ain't gonna cut it, amigo. I gotta see him, in person, to make sure it's all worked out."

"He's not available. Let me know what you want and I'll work it out with him."

"Hey, man, we . . . I gotta see him, *in person,* you know?"

"Give me your number and I'll get back to you."

What the fuck? O.K., he'll give him the number of one of the cells for his clients.

"Listen, this is some serious shit. You better get me the info where he's at in the next 24 hours, or there'll be consequences, like people getting hurt, you know?"

Ralph hung up.

Manny El Bronx looked at his cell phone like it had just dissed him.

That was two days ago. Manny hadn't heard from the university guy. But he called Papo anyway to tell him the mule was back on the island. The professor asshole didn't say no.

He hurried out of his house, got into his Lexus and drove to the airport to pick up those two guys. Maybe he shouldn't have told Papo that he knew where this fuckin guy was. Well, actually all he said was "the mule is back on the island and now we can fix up everything."

"Get him, get what he owes us, or crack him open," Papo said. "I'm gonna send some help."

"I don't know if I need . . ."

"I'm sending my guys."

So it looked like Papo didn't trust him to do it himself. That's O.K., nobody believed the kid's story about the packets of *perico*. They still believed he tried to steal ten packets.

Next conversation with Papo, this is what he'd say: "I should have been standing over him when he swallowed the stuff, even though it happened in the D.R., but I trusted him before and he never shorted us. This ain't gonna happen again, Papo, you can take my word on that."

Fuckin mule. Trying to fuck us up! Well, he'll come through with the money for what he stole or get what he deserves.

We may have to lean on that professor asshole too.

SIXTEEN

We were skip-counting by twos, learning even and odd numbers, simple fractions, all about insects, what magnets do and why, how all the suns, moons, planets, and stars move, when to capitalize, how to look up words in the dictionary. We were also writing in cursive and reading *Las Aventuras de Juan Bobo*. Sister Margaret came to the classes every day for the first week or so, to see how I was doing. She said it's going well, I should just keep following the lesson plans made by Sister Gloria before she got locked up.

The kids were great. They came to school bursting with energy and ready to learn. They couldn't wait until I took them out to the small field behind the school during recess. I got both the boys and girls to take part in relay races and they were screaming while passing sticks and dropping them and picking them up again. The parents went out of their way to help around the school—cooking, cleaning, fixing up and painting—and I started to give evening classes once a week to the older people in the barrio who had never learned to read or write. *Doña* Belén, the great-grandmother of Patricia, one of my second-grade students, took the evening class. *Doña* Belén and Patricia read to each other every night after Patricia corrected her *bisabuela's* homework.

Both Sister Margaret and Sister Ana Maria were terrific. Sister Ana Maria, nearly eighty, tall and bent with thinning white hair on a very pink scalp, had agreed to come down from the states to teach kindergarten and first-grade while I taught second and Sister Margaret took care of the third graders. Both nuns were New Yorkers. Sister Ana Maria had left Puerto Rico when she was ten years old. Both were fervent baseball fans, though they were more attuned to the old times. During the first days of school, I was invited to join them for lunch in the small school cafeteria and, probably for my benefit, they picked up on the same argument they must have had for decades. Brooklyn Dodger fan Sister Margaret said Jackie Robinson was the most exciting player ever— "When he reached first base, it was like the coming of Advent, the knowing of the miracles of the past, the longing, the expectation, the anticipation of stolen bases in the immediate future, forgive me, Jesus" (she would cross herself)—and Sister Ana Maria, who'd rooted for the New York Giants, would reply: "Two words, sister. Willie Mays. I need say no more."

It was as though the Dodgers and Giants had never deserted for California.

I called my Mom to let her know I had a teacher's job.

"Where?"

"Up in the mountains."

"Where up in the mountains?"

"Near Jayuya.

I'll see you soon. Really."

"When?"

"Soon."

"Why couldn't I reach you by your cell phone?"

"I lost it. I'll give you the number as soon as I get a new phone."

"When will that be?"

"Soon."

A long, deep sigh. "O.K., mi'jo. As long as you are well. You are well, right?"

"I'm fine. Please don't worry. Everything is going good."

It was going O.K. for me. But of course, not everything was upbeat, especially in such a poor barrio in Puerto Rico in the year 2000. Many of the homes were no more than wooden shacks perched on stilts on the hillsides of tangled trees, shrubs and vines. There were a few businesses on the main street: Pucho's colmado, Ferdie's hardware and lumber, Kiko's *Cuchifritos* (fried food) stand, the Super Star video store, and a kiosk to buy lottery tickets. Almost no one had jobs. But no one was starving either because of food stamps. Some of the older kids were into drugs and too many of the out-of-work husbands fueled their frustrations with rum and took off from their wives and kids. More than a few "nervous" people wandered around the barrio when they should have been getting medicine or treatment. But almost nobody stole and most of the people helped each other out, which the poor seem to do more than others.

I actually got a check after the first week, courtesy, I believe of the prof, and it was enough to stock up on food for a while. In those first days, I spent my free time reading and writing in my journal. Also, I was thinking up other ways to get money for the Laura Rosario Scholarship. I thought of going to the press before turning myself in to confess to my drug-running activities. I wouldn't name any of the others, but I'd tell the reporters I'd be willing to go to prison if my story got out and maybe people would contribute to the scholarship fund.

That was just one of my stupid ideas. But I wasn't going to let Laura down!

One night, soon after I started at the school, I met Julia.

By 10 p.m., most of the people in the barrio were sleeping, but four or five guys would still be in Puchi's colmado, drinking beer and shouting at each other like they were the last people remaining in Puerto Rico. I saw and heard them on my usual walk before going to bed.

I was going down the main street, the only paved road in town, accompanied by a mangy mutt who latched on to me during my walks a couple of nights before when I gave it some soda crackers I was carrying home from Puchi's. I was passing the shuttered lottery kiosk when the shouts started coming from a shack at the foot of the hill. I heard stuff banging in the house, then a woman came running out with a crying little boy. A skinny guy stumbled after them, cursing to the heavens.

The woman almost ran into me, then ducked behind me with her little boy. The drunken guy reached around and grabbed her by the hair and started tugging her away while the little kid sat on the ground bawling his heart out.

"Hey, let her go!" I shouted.

The guy looked at me like I just landed from Mars. The woman used his distraction to smash him in the face with her fist. He let go of her for just a brief moment, then grabbed her around the throat. I had no choice but to jump on the guy's back and put my arms around his neck and pull him off the woman. He gave way fairly easily. The mutt was barking and growling around the guy. Then he stood, slapped at his jeans, looked at me like he thought I was nuts for interfering in a domestic dispute. Then he kicked at the dog, missed, spat at me, turned and left.

"Cobarde!" the woman yelled at his back.

"Puta!" He yelled while still walking away with a half-limp. The woman went to the little boy and picked him up. "It's O.K., it's O.K.," she told the boy. "The monster is gone."

Which is just what I had learned to call my drunken father. I remembered the sonovabitch beating my mother, and smacking me around, though I also remembered Mom landing a couple of good punches which made his nose bleed.

I was choking and Mom pulled me out of bed and out the back kitchen door and the flames were bursting out the windows. He had lit the gas that he spilled from the olive-colored canister he kept in his pickup. It was in the middle of the night and we wandered from our barrio into the city. We sat on the steps to the Arecibo city hall through the night, until Mom's cousin Sonia came to work in the morning and they went to the bank and then her cousin drove us all the way to the airport in San Juan and we got on a plane for New York, no luggage, no nothing. Then the rats on the pipes overhead when we stayed in that basement because Mom didn't know her friend in the building was in Puerto Rico and we couldn't get into her apartment, and I clubbed the shit out of the rats, maybe thinking I was bashing in the head of my old man.

I was always scared of him, hoping he would not come home and when he did, hating his guts. He must have done a couple of decent things toward me and my mother or she wouldn't have stayed with him the ten years she did. But I really couldn't remember any of them, I must have blocked them out.

O.K., he took me to Winter League ballgames and for the first time, I saw Bernie Williams play for the Caguas Criollos. O.K., when he was sober he'd show me the medals he won in Vietnam and tell me all these war stories and these funny stories about his job as an orderly at the VA hospital, where he said the psychiatrists were crazier than the patients. That was when he was sober.

Now I was hating this other fuckin drunk monster who seemed like a puny jerk but scared the hell out of his kid and his wife. The woman had a long, thin face with high cheekbones, a small pointy nose, a jutting dimpled chin, and dark brown eyes. Her black hair was cut abruptly at her shoulders like she had gotten mad at it one day for something.

I went with her and her kid back to their house. She thanked me and cried and I patted her arm and went home. She found out where I lived and the next night came to see me. She brought me a homemade *flan de coco* but refused my invitation to come in. She said no one was watching her little boy.

She returned the following night and said a neighbor was watching the kid. I made coffee through a coffee sock and we ate the *flan.*

Julia's four-year-old son was her second child. A little girl died five years ago soon after birth.

"I will die myself first before I let anyone hurt Pedrito," she said, her lips trembling.

She was a teenager when she had her first child, so I figured she was a couple of years older than me. She was pretty and had a very nice figure, though curvier on the bottom than full on top.

Her great-grandparents, who had come to the island from Spain and Lebanon, were poor merchants. "All the family, we were always poor," she said. "But most were good people. My parents, their parents, they worked so hard, in the fields, in the city. But that *cabrón* (her husband), he's nothing more than a miserable drunken bum. I hope and I pray every day that he does what he is always saying, to borrow money from his brother in Chicago for a plane ticket to join him there. I pray, my God, that he goes and rots there."

This "monster" wasn't her legal husband. "He is Pedritos father, but he has deserted us many times. just came back two days ago and always has been drunk and has made me . . . forced himself on me. I hate him!"

She didn't stay long that night. But she returned to my house a couple of nights later with *asopao de pollo,* chicken gumbo, Puerto Rican-style. I had a bottle of Spanish red wine I had brought up with me from the city and we drank the whole bottle. Then, before at least I knew it, we were tangled up on my bed. She made love with a vengeance that sort of shook me up but in a good way. After, she took the medal Laura had given me in her long, thin fingers and studied it.

"You are a good Catholic?" she asked.

"No," I answered. "I wear this as a reminder of someone." I felt the flush of guilt, then sadness.

"But you should not wear something which says you are a religious person if you are not."

She seemed sort of angry. What the hell?

I didn't argue. I just felt guilty the next few nights when we continued to make love. But the guilt had nothing to do with the medal or with religion, or my lack of it.

Julia didn't smile much. She was stubborn about what she believed.

"Rats are children of the Devil," she once said after we saw one skirting along the floor of my shack and I picked up my Louisville Slugger to smack it out the front door.

I laughed. She didn't.

She said one night: "The hearts of all those who have died within one year of the Second Coming will start beating again in the grave, and those who are dug up will live a second life."

"How do they get the message out that they're alive again?"

"Soon people will know about this."

More than once, she said, "We are only here on earth to suffer."

"Suffering is just one part of life," I told her. "There are lots of things to enjoy while you're alive."

She said nothing. Then she gave me a rare smile and I saw the spark of lust and maybe a little love in her eyes.

SEVENTEEN

Chucho gripped the armrests as the jet, rumbling down the runway, picked up speed, faster, faster, shaking, rattling—*lift the fuck off, get up, up!*—finally separating from the ground, wheels slamming into the body, curving toward the sky, taking away his breath.

He hated fuckin flying! As soon as he could he'd order a rum and Coke.

Junior, in the window seat next to Chucho, peered out at the boats on Jamaica Bay. The waterfront houses were now the size of the bungalows on a Monopoly board. Gray clouds suddenly blocked out all views. The plane was climbing, climbing, then leveling off under a solid blue canopy, white pillow clouds sculpted below.

Chucho couldn't wait to get his hands on that fucker who gave him a broken nose and made him get stitches and now made him get on this fuckin shaking jet bouncing from side to side. He'd gladly carve up that fucker. He pinged one of the buttons above his seat. Where was the goddamn waitress? He needed a drink, bad.

Their trip to Puerto Rico and their "mission" once they got there saddened Junior. He always felt sad when he returned to the island. He wasn't sure why. Maybe the memories. Which, however, weren't all that bad. Sure the family had been poor. Yeah, he grew up in a funky barrio near the Martín Peña Channel. But he had plenty of friends, enough rice and beans and even got lots of A's up to high school. Then the family decided to move to New York. Pop José Sr., working his ass off in bottling plants in Jersey. Papi, Mami, Abuela Rosa, him, his three sisters and two brothers, in a shitty apartment with three tiny bedrooms on East 103rd Street. Still, A's and B's in high school, a couple of years at Boricua College, going for a degree in civil and structural engineering. Put up bridges and buildings, pull down big bucks.

Shit, he couldn't stick around for four more years, including grad school. The money was in the streets. Friends of friends hooked him up with Papo in the Bronx. He did get into the building, after all—building his own bank account, with something left over for the family. More than they ever had before, so he didn't want to hear no complaints. Didn't get many either. Except from Eduardo. Now a Pentecostal minister, preaching in the streets and storefronts of El Barrio and the Bronx. Good luck, bro. Don't fuck it up for me, I won't tell on you. Unless you already "confessed." The *perico* you introduced me to when I was your 14-year-old kid brother. No problem. You preach the good life, I'll practice it.

So why the sadness on the trip back to the island? Because he remembered to remember.

Big bro Eduardo, taking him to the beach, teaching him how to swim, helping him pick up girls, showing him everything, from how to throw a curve ball to how to jack off. Also slapping him around when he didn't get how to do things just right. Big bro, now chewing out Junior whenever they meet for doing the work of the Devil. *Fuck it!* Fuck you, Eddie and fuck the fuckin Devil.

And Delia, she was the last person he wanted to run into. Probably shooting up somewhere in Barrio Obrero, where he heard she'd moved in with some guy. Thank God their kids were back in New York with his parents.

Milly and Lilly, the twins. Living with his parents until he gets a big enough house, somewhere in Queens, and brings everyone there. Get a real *novia*. Live like a real family.

He'd make the phone call right after they checked in. Hopefully, it'll lead them quickly to the mule, so they won't have to screw around. The kid's back on the island, according to that Manny guy.

Junior checked his cell phone to see the numbers copied off the kid's cell.

We'll lean hard on this Richie until he comes up with lots of bills, or, as Papo says, we'll cut off some fingers and toes, break some arms and legs, smash a head, slice off balls, cut out a heart, whatthefuckever it'll take for him to learn what it means to cross Papo.

He felt both a twitching sadness and—he admitted it—a tingling joy when he had to do these things. Sado-maso-whatever.

"What the fuck was that?" asked Chucho, jerking his head around the cabin in all directions.

"Just some turbulence," said Junior, as a ping introduced a sugary voice reminding passengers to refasten their seatbelts. "It happens on every flight."

This was Chucho's second flight. He didn't remember the first one when he was three-months-old. That was twenty-fuckin'-five years ago when the family flew up to the states. He didn't know shit about Puerto Rico and he didn't want to know. What he wanted was to be another Papo, a fuckin king, sending his underlings down to Mexico or out to Chicago or to Florida or PR to take care of *his* business. He wouldn't take shit from anybody. Snap his fingers and have the fuckers wiped out.

The plane was actually rattling! "I want another drink," said Chucho. "Where the fuck is the waitress?"

"She's the stewardess. Calm down!"

"Fuck it, I got to piss." Chucho undid his seat belt and staggered and swayed down the aisle.

Jackass. More trouble than he's worth. Junior didn't know why Papo kept him on. One day, he's gonna do something that'll fuck up not only himself but the rest of us.

Junior liked to do business with guys, like himself, who knew how to keep their cool. Maybe he could ditch the asshole after they landed in PR. Work with just the contact there.

Naw, Papo would get pissed. Chucho, he said, reminded him of one of his sons, the kid who was sent up for trying to rob a bank. Another Einstein, he tried to shoot his way out against a couple of bank guards until his handgun, made in Brazil and bought off a junkie in the projects, exploded in his hand.

Chucho returned. "Where's the wait . . . whatever the fuck she is."

The stewardess finally appeared. The turbulence had died down. "May I help you, sir?

"Yeah, bring me all the goddamn rum you got in the plane."

Three double drinks later the plane started descending. Chucho white-knuckled the armrests.

Junior looked out at clusters of shacks, then high-rise buildings, then bulky white oceanfront hotels, broad beaches, dark blue water, white caps and a wavy sudsy line of foam. Then tall downtown buildings, a long line of cars that didn't seem to be moving, grassy areas, shacks, waterway, grassy area leading to the runway and—bump, zoom, louder zoom ("What the *fuck*?" from Chucho) –the jet coasted to a terminal.

"Fuck!" said Chucho. "My ears are filled with cement. "O.K.," he said, "let's get this shit over with."

EIGHTEEN

On the weekend, we took a public van into Ponce on the south coast. Pedrito was with us. He was an incredibly quiet kid with large dark eyes that looked startled when they stared at anything. We went to the big shopping mall to look at all the luxurious items no one in our barrio could afford. I bought Julia a short-sleeved red blouse which she insisted on wearing right away, putting her loose white top in the bag from the store. She was wearing a black skirt and heels and the tight blouse gave her a really attractive look. Pedrito got a toy helicopter that flew by remote control. Then we went to Burger King in the food court. It left me with about ten dollars. But I had enough food in the house for the week.

I had promised the prof and his wife that I would more or less stay put until they contacted me, but I really didn't expect to run into any trouble in this mall or in this city the other side of the island.

That's what I thought.

After visiting the mall, we took a *público* back to the city's main plaza and got *piraguas* from a cart and we headed to the red-and-black-striped firehouse museum there. "I match," said Julia, looking down at her red blouse and tight black skirt, one of the few times I heard her make some sort of

joke.

Pedrito's eye bulged at the fire engines and the fire-fighting equipment. "I want to be a fireman," he announced.

A typical Saturday afternoon "family" outing.

We were on our way to the terminal to get another *público* back to our barrio when the guy called out to us. He was on a bench in front of the terminal. Julia cursed and took Pedrito's hand and grabbed me by the arm.

It was her "husband." He said something to two other guys who were sitting on the bench. He pushed himself off the bench and weaved across the street. He had a look on his face like he was about to say or do something he found distasteful, but that had to be done. He stood in front of us, still weaving. He looked deep at Julia, down at Pedrito and ignored me.

"What are you doin' here, woman!" It wasn't a question.

Julia said nothing. She pulled Pedrito along, letting go of my arm.

The guy blocked Julia's way. "I ask you something. Answer me, woman!"

"Get out of my way," Julia said.

The guy looked as disheveled and as drunk as the night when I'd first seen him. "Why ain't you home taking care of the house and our little boy here, instead of walking around so everyone can see you all dressed up like a *puta,*" he said.

"Hey!" I said.

The guy blinked me away. "*Puta!*" he shouted at Julia. "*Puta! Whore!*"

A crowd was beginning to gather. Some of them had little smiles on their faces.

"Get out of my way!" Julia shouted again as her "husband" kept blocking her path. She pushed him in the chest. Two young guys in the crowd began to hoot.

I started over to him. His two companions, who looked in no better shape than their friend, came over from the bench and took my arms and pulled me back. I started wrestling with them. Pedrito began crying. The women in the crowd put out their hands, reaching out to the boy. "*Pobrecito*" they kept saying.

The crowd was encircling us. "This woman, who's worth nothing," said Julia's supposed mate, "is the daughter of the great whore. She sleeps with anyone with balls."

"Except you," said a young fellow in the crowd, drawing laughs.

"Who said that?"

As soon as he turned his head to the crowd, it happened. A dull gleam, then a quick slash.

There was a long high shriek. The guy's face turned white, then purple and blood seemed to pump out of his sliced cheek. He put a hand to his cheek, drew his fingers down over the wound, looked at his blood-dripping fingers with angry disgust, as though those fingers had slashed the skin. He ripped off his filthy gray-white shirt and put it against the wound. His ribs stuck out. Julia dropped the straight razor to the ground, tightened the hold on her son's hand and pushed her way through the shocked crowd.

Someone screamed: "Call the police!" But no one moved and Julia quickly disappeared. The guy's two companions let me go and went up to their friend. He kept dabbing the shirt against his cheek while grabbing the arm of one of his friends and holding on to it.

"Get me to the hospital!" the guy said. "Come on! I'm bleeding to death!"

The crowd parted as his friends led him down the street, drops of blood soaking through the shirt and dripping behind him.

We got back to the barrio in separate public vans. That evening, Julia came to my house, tearing up as she told me that she was sure that the guy was about to beat her and their son right there on the crowded street. She would not take him hitting her or the boy one more time. She said she started carrying the razor the night after we met, in case "that *cabrón*" ever attacked again."

What Julia did was shocking, but who could say the guy didn't deserve it?

One thing I did know is that our "relationship" couldn't deepen on my part. No, I wasn't afraid of angering Julia. But I knew I could never love her. Not in any deep, lasting way.

What I didn't want to do is cause her more hurt. I would see her less, gradually break it off.

No police appeared in the next few days. Nor did the guy.

But other things began to happen that got me ready to go on the run again.

NINETEEN

"Your argument holds no weight in this court. The transfer of these lands to the Navy was legal and above-board. The land is needed for national defense. *Licenciado*, you really should read the laws regarding property rights, not to mention Public Law 600, which details the relationship between the United States and Puerto Rico and points to the responsibilities of the island toward the national defense. I suggest you go back to the basics, study them, then, if you wish, return to the court with a cogent and coherent argument."

As Tere had been warned, U.S. District Judge Peter Maldonado really was a sonovabitch. Just a week ago he had dismissed the Legal Services class action drawn up by Tere to stop the Vieques bombing. Maldonado upheld the U.S. government's "sovereign immunity," a defense based on the medieval concept that "the king can do no wrong." In other words, you can't sue the government to stop it from bombing wherever the hell it wants to because of a concept developed in the enlightened Middle Ages. Now Maldonado chewed out Tere as only an arrogant judge would berate a lowly *abogada* from Legal Services. Well, the hell with him, she would continue with her defense of the 32 women—nuns, nurses, housewives, teachers, lawyers. By being arrested for their protest on the Navy firing range, they at least put a temporary halt to the maneuvers, even though they'd been locked up and remained in jail and the maneuvers started up again.

"But, your honor," Tere went on, "there is a precedent for the defense known as justification, necessity, choice of evils. As quoted in *People v. Strock, Colorado, 1981* and *People v. Trujillo, Colorado, 1984*, this doctrine exonerates a person who has to choose between two imminent evils, and who has no lawful means of avoiding the greater one. The defendants here had to choose between breaking the law of trespass or preventing further damage to the environment by the only means available to them. For more than fifty years, the Navy has dropped bombs and set-off explosives on this very small island. It has experimented with Agent Orange, depleted uranium, cyanide. It has threatened the health and well-being of the nine thousand residents there. The maneuvers have contaminated the environment, poisoning the waters, caused cancer and breathing problems. The Navy has . . ." "Yeah, yeah, we've heard all that hundreds of times and it's still irrelevant," interrupted Judge Maldonado. "You cannot violate the law for the sake of your own belief or to advance a cause. This is exactly what the defendants have done. Let them use lawful alternatives if they want to test a policy of the U.S. government."

Maldonado's small, dimpled chin shook. He pursed his lips, then pushed back his horn-rimmed glasses. He reached under his black robe for a white handkerchief and wiped his mouth.

Tere looked around. The courtroom in Old San Juan was packed with relatives and friends of the accused, and others opposed to the Navy bombing. Several reporters sat in the first rows. The air-conditioning was barely working and it was hot as hell. Tere was sweating in her neck-high white blouse and newly bought dark blue pants suit.

"Your honor, the court should realize that Puerto Rico is not a full part of the U.S. democratic system. We have no voting legislators in Congress and cannot vote for the commander-in-chief who sends our young men to fight and die in U.S. wars. How else can national officials be made fully aware of the situation of the people on Vieques without 'illegal' protests on the Navy's firing range there?"

"Irrelevant," said Maldonado. "We're not here today to argue about Puerto Rico's relationship with the United States. We're here because these people broke the law. That's all there is to it."

A moan came from the spectators. Maldonado smashed down his gavel. "I don't want any displays of emotion! I'll clear this courtroom if I have to!"

The judge took out his handkerchief again, took off his glasses, wiped them, put the handkerchief back under his robe with one hand, replaced his glasses with the other hand, and said, "I sentence the defendants to sixty days in prison, minus the ten days already served. I also fine each defendant $1,000, to be paid within thirty days of their release from prison."

There was a shocked hush in the court. Tere shook her head, frowned and blew air out of the side of her mouth.

The judge's dimpled chin quaked. "If you don't like the decision, *licenciada,* you can appeal it. But I don't want any displays of dissatisfaction while these court proceedings are continuing. I have not dismissed the court yet. I have a good mind to hold you in contempt."

Tere said nothing.

Judge Maldonado smacked down his gavel. He took a quick exit through a door behind the bench.

The relatives and friends hugged Tere and thanked her for what they said was, despite the judge's terrible ruling, an inspiring defense. They would form a group to try to raise the money for the fines. Tere found the fines outrageous. Many of these women could not even afford bail. As they were being led away, several of the women, in orange jumpsuits, raised their left fists.

Tere left the courtroom frustrated and deeply depressed. The bombing continued, the protestors remained in prison. Two staggering losses in a row. Maybe, she told herself, she should return to what might be her true calling: owner-operator of the Wishy Washy Laundromat.

After coming home, Tere told Ralph about the latest court defeat for the Vieques protestors. "That judge, Maldonado, is really a sonovabitch. He said my argument was irrelevant . . . I felt like telling him to . . ."

Ralph tried for as sympathetic a look as he could muster. He knew Tere was shaken by the verdicts and wondered whether to tell her about the phone call. He decided he had to, for Richie's sake. He left out the "people getting hurt" threat. "Is there any way we could get the D.A. or someone to arrange protection for Richie without giving them the whole story?"

"I don't see how," said Tere.

"What the hell can we do?"

"I don't know" Tere looked irritated.

He'd have to get word to Richie about the phone call. To tell him what? Continue to lay low? Make some sort of payoff? Go to the authorities? Settle in San Francisco or Madrid or Buenos Aires?

Over dinner, Diana said: "A couple of the boys in my class said they tried pot, which they got on the beach in Condado, it was awesome. I'm thirteen and like you said, I'm mature for my age, so how come you won't let me smoke some pot, just to try it? If I'm going to be an artist . . ."

"Cut it out!" Ralph said.

His daughter looked down, hurt.

He felt bad. What was he supposed to say, "Save the roach for me"?

Later, Tere told Ralph she would talk to some people in her office about Richie's problem, without mentioning his name or giving personal details.

"I'm sorry, I wasn't too helpful before, but I was so pissed at that judge; he spoke to me like I was just out of law school. Hey, I'm sorry."

"Come on. You don't have to apologize. The *independentistas* call that judge a *pitiyanqui*, always ruling in favor of the U.S. government."

Before she went to bed, Ralph stopped Diana, took her hand and hugged her tightly. Her skin was cool from the shower she'd just taken and she smelled of the special lavender soap she used. Her short, curly black hair was damp and left a wet spot on the shoulder of his shirt. She pulled her head back and Ralph continued to hold her hand and looked into those deep, clear, innocent, approval-seeking brown eyes.

"You're a beautiful daughter and you're going to be a great artist and as soon as you get to be forty-five you can smoke all the pot you want. Now kiss me good night."

Diana returned her old man's hug and kisses.

Tere called it a night after the eleven o'clock news, right after a report on the judge's decision on Vieques.

Tomorrow, he'd see an old friend about Richie.

TWENTY

"Is this the mother of Richie Pérez?"

"That's right. Who is this?"

"How do you do, ma'am. Permit me to introduce myself. I'm Celestino Ortiz, an old friend of Richie's from Morris High School, we played on the baseball team together. Richie told me if I ever got to Puerto Rico, which I just have on a two-week vacation with my new bride, we were just married last week, he said I should look him up, which I would like to do. The only thing, I've been calling his cell phone and getting no reply and I have no other number for him. Richie told me that you worked at Arecibo City Hall. I hope you don't mind, I looked up the number and I called and was told by the operator that you had finished working for the day, so I told her about my attempt to reach your son and she kindly looked up your home number and gave it to me. By the way, I'm calling from the Caribe Hilton Hotel, where Anita and I are honeymooning. It really is a beautiful hotel."

Don't overdo it.

"I don't know how you can get in touch with him," said Richie's mother. "He just started teaching in a school up in the mountains, near Jayuya. I don't have any further information for you, I'm sorry."

"How about the name of the school?"

"I don't even know that. I'm so sorry. When Richie calls again, which he should be doing soon, I'll let him know that you called and that you and your bride are staying at the Caribe Hilton. What's the name again?"

"My name?"

"Yes."

Shit!

"Umm . . . Celestino. Umm . . . Ortiz. Celestino Ortiz."

Junior was calling from a public phone at the Caribe Hilton, although they were staying at Papo's brother-in-law's guesthouse down the street. The mother's numbers were on Richie's cell phone. A news story Richie carried in his confiscated wallet reported that as the center fielder for Morris High he'd hit two home runs and two doubles in a game against DeWitt Clinton.

"If you want to find someone in Puerto Rico who's on the run," Papo had said, "call the mother. Even if the guy is a mass murderer. Especially if he's a mass murderer—he'll go home to Mami."

Well, at least they now knew the general area where they could search for the mule. Junior didn't think it would be too difficult to find the sonovabitch now.

"No problem," Manny El Bronx told Junior and Chucho. They were seated at a table with a view of the ocean outside El Hamburger. The sky was a seamless bleached blue. A long, black container ship appeared motionless on the sun-hazed horizon.

Manny said: "I know a guy who's got a cousin who works for the Department of Education who can get us the names and locations of all the schools around Jayuya, which ain't a big town, but it's way up in the mountains."

Chucho bit into his burger. Relish and ketchup dribbled from the side of his mouth.

"Wipe your mouth," Junior said, narrowing his small eyes to hyphens.

Chucho wiped the side of his mouth and his chin with the back of his hand.

"What the fuck you got a napkin for?"

"To blow my nose," said Chucho, who did just that, then looked into the napkin to see what he'd collected.

Junior shook his head in disgust. Since the plane ride, just about everything Chucho was doing pissed Junior off. He wasn't crazy about this Manny El Bronx asshole either.

Turning to Manny, he said, "I thought you said you knew where this guy was. We ain't here to run around the fuckin island trying to chase this guy down."

"Hey, I told Papo I found out that the mule was back on the island, which he is. Then you guys appeared before I actually pinned him down. Take a couple of days at the beach while I find out the school where he's at. "

Manny thought: Will that fuckin professor at the University call him back? Should he call again, make a real threat? Better not, not right now. Check out the schools first. Manny hoped his earlier call to the professor didn't cause the prof to warn the kid. About what? Well, it was stupid of him to make a sort-of threat to the professor. Maybe if he didn't follow up on it with another call, the mule would stay in place. And they'd be able to get to him. And get what they wanted. Then those two could go the fuck back to the states, and he'd be able to resume his business. Build a better life for himself and Manny Jr.

"I'll get on this to find the school as soon as we finish these burgers," Manny said.

"These beat Big Macs by a mile," Chucho said, shoving a second hamburger into his mouth.

Choke on it, said Junior under his breath.

"What I can do for you is to send up a couple of Close Protection officers. They'll be really low-profile, but they'll still be watching out for the threat and ensuring that your guy is protected at all times. Listen, Ralph, I owe you one from that time in Jersey, and there's going to be no charge for now. But from what you told me, I think you've got to get these guys arrested or get this young fellow off the island, far away, you know?"

Ralph nodded. He knew. Sitting on the other side of Roberto's uncluttered desk, in the Roberto Betancourt Security Company's frosty air-conditioned office, Ralph said: "Roberto, I appreciate your help. I'll contact the young fellow to let him know the protection is available. I'll get back to you as soon as I get his OK."

"Fine. I just want you to know again that I appreciate what you did for us."

"How's Wanda?"

"She's fine, thanks. Like I told you, it was a slow process, but she remembers everything now. Even the guy who knocked her over the head and stole the car and how she wandered into the wilds of Newark and Elizabeth and the other places before you found her in Trenton. We got to get together again, you and Tere and us. Let's make a dinner date soon."

Ralph nodded again. "O.K., that would be great." Or would it? Whenever she saw her "rescuer" Wanda's eyes filled and she seemed to come on to him, especially during the after-dinner drinks. It had made for a couple of uncomfortable evenings after Roberto had moved his security business to the island.

Ralph stood. "So you have most of the information, right?"

"Yeah, sure," Roberto said, checking his computer screen. "Just give me a call and we'll take care of the kid."

Once home, Ralph made several calls to Richie's school. The phone was either not answered or he got messages that it was not in service. He called the phone company. They told him the school phone was not in service.

The next day the phone was working—barely. He told Richie through incredible static that he wanted to send up protection for him because . . .

. . . The phone went dead. Ralph drummed his fingers on his desk and took very deep breaths.

TWENTY-ONE

They rented the two-door white Mazda, figuring it would be practically unnoticeable. Junior drove, Chucho rode shotgun and Manny sat in the back, talking on his cell phone to his various guys in the projects, instructing them which of the underlings could and couldn't be trusted at the *puntos* during the one night or maybe two he wouldn't be around.

Junior blamed their late start—it was three in the afternoon—on Chucho, who slept until noon and kept going to the toilet. Chucho said the Puerto Rican fried food had fucked up his stomach. Like Junior didn't see him always eating fast-food crap in New York. What a pain in the ass this little fucker was.

They climbed the narrow roads to Jayuya. Small concrete houses sat just off the sides of the road; wooden shacks on stilts were perched precariously on steep inclines. Then they saw jagged limestone cliffs, then broad valleys and hillsides with houses jutting from them, then mist-covered mountains and huge shiny white clouds that looked like painted, pasted-on cutouts. They were moving past the tropical forest, into the Cordillera Central.

Junior remembered riding through the mountains as a kid with his family for Christmas visits to relatives in Adjuntas.

The whole family at Tío Gregorio's farm. Aunts, uncles, cousins, great-this-and-thats, crawling babies, wrinkled ancients. The pig is roasting on the spit, the adults are getting happy on the coquito. *Me, my brothers and sisters, we're kids running like mad over the fields, breathing air that didn't stink like the air on the edge of the stinking channel in the stinking barrio in the middle of the city.*

Chucho hung out the window, taking in the incredible scenery. He ducked back when the road got even narrower and more twisted. Trucks and cars came around the blind turns blowing their horns.

"Holy shit!" said Chucho. "What a place! Where are we, in Switzerland minus snow, or something? I thought PRs only lived in the slums in big cities."

"You got a lot to fuckin learn," said Junior.

"Yeah, I know there's things I don't know about. But at least I don't make believe I know when I don't know."

"If you don't know shit, how would you know that the people who say they know, don't really know what they're talking about?"

"I can tell. Lots of people make believe they know things which they don't."

"No shit," said Junior.

"Yeah, no shit," said Chucho.

The sun, huge and orange, was gliding behind a mountain with three peaks when they reached Jayuya.

"You got the list?" Junior asked Manny.

"Yeah, but it's too late to start today."

"I wonder why," said Junior, glaring at Chucho.

"Hey, I was sick, you know? What the fuck you want?"

"Let me see the directions for the guest house," Manny said as he turned a sheet of paper with the list of the twelve public schools in Jayuya to a hand-drawn map on the other side. Manny got the list from one of his guy's sisters who worked at the Education Department. The map was sketched by the sister's husband, who booked rooms for them at the guesthouse owned by his great uncle.

Manny directed Junior up, down and through the town for about half an hour. Each dead-end brought a "What the fuck?!" from Manny while Junior gnashed his teeth. They cruised down a dirt road at the other end of town and were soon by a stream that led to a river. A simple two-story wooden house with a small front porch and two small balconies stood above the river. The only sounds were the slight rippling of the river and some hens clucking in the back of the house. The house had a front and rear view of high green hills and higher brown mountains. A sign hanging from the porch roof said: *Casa de la Libertasd.*

"Here it is!" said Manny. "Boy, that asshole drew a real shitty map."

House of Freedom, strange name for a guesthouse, thought Junior. Still, maybe it was a portent of things to come. Freedom was just what he wanted from these two jerkoffs.

"*Buenas noches, compañeros.* I am Raphael del Valle."

The tall, erect old man, dressed in a long-sleeve white guayabera, had a full head of wavy white hair. He stood on the top steps of the porch, his arms outstretched. He must have heard them driving up. "Carlito called to tell me you would be here and I've reserved one very large room for you with two beds and a cot. Please, enter." He swept his arms toward the front door.

Junior popped the trunk and they picked up overnight bags. The evening mountain air was surprisingly cool. They nodded as they passed the old guy and went inside. A short round woman with long white hair piled on top of her head and held there by sparkling combs and clips smiled at them from behind a desk in a small makeshift receiving area. A large Puerto Rican flag was tacked to the wall behind the desk.

The old guy announced: "This is Rosa, for the past fifty years my wife. *Mi amor*, please register these gentlemen and give them the key to their room. Before you go upstairs, perhaps you will join us in the reception room"—he pointed to a curtained area off to the side— "for a welcome drink, which is on the house."

They signed in—Manny as Juan García and Junior as Francisco González. Chucho stood blinking down on the register page until Junior told him: "Hey, José López, did you forget your name?"

"Hey, "said Chucho, "I don't like . . ."

"Just put your goddamn name down there, José López!" Junior said.

Chucho finally signed in with the alias and Junior took the key. He also picked up a map of Jayuya from several tourist brochures in a rack.

The old guy pulled the heavy red curtain back to reveal the reception room. The room was crowded with rattan furniture, potted palms, bookcases and, on the walls, framed photos, and prints. The pictures all had Puerto Rico independence themes— portraits of Nineteenth-Century patriots with long beards and drooping mustaches; news photos of people Junior recognized, like Nationalist Party leader Pedro Albizu Campos making a hand-waving speech, and a newspaper photo of the Nationalists who shot up Congress being put under arrest. There was one really big print of an attractive, dark-haired, dark-eyed, woman superimposed on the Puerto Rican flag.

"That woman," said Raphael del Valle, "is my cousin Blanca Canales, who spent her life working to free her country and actually led the revolt here in Jayuya in 1950, in which myself and Rosa, we proudly participated, until the Americanos ordered the National Guard troops to invade our city. Look, there is a photo over there of the soldiers marching through our streets with their rifles at the ready. Here is a photo of the wreckage caused by the U.S. planes, P-47 Thunderbolts, which actually dropped bombs onto the city, and by the artillery that was fired on us.

"But before that, we captured the police station and we marched to the plaza where Blanca declared the Free Republic of Puerto Rico. I helped to raise the flag of our nation in the plaza, the flag which we were not permitted to display at that time."

"No shit," said Chucho.

Junior, Chucho, and Manny sat on rockers around the room while Del Valle sat on the edge of a small bamboo-framed couch. A girl of about twenty in a black blouse and jeans came into the room carrying a tray holding four tall brown liquid-and-ice-filled glasses. When she leaned over to offer the drinks, Chucho and Manny snuck glances down the front of her blouse, then winked at each other. Junior thought she was a knockout.

"This drink, my friends," said Del Valle, "is the house specialty. Rum aged at least 10 years in an old barrel, mixed with some lime juice, brown sugar, and soda. I call it a Puerto Rico Libre."

Then the old guy said: *"Salud, dinero, amor y libertad!"*

Junior and his cohorts half-heartedly lifted their glasses, then drank.

"Umh, just right!" said Del Valle. "Not too sweet, not too sour. You have become an expert, *mi vida*," Del Valle said to the young woman, who beamed.

"This is my granddaughter, Natasha," the old guy said. "She is an honors student at the University, studying to be a doctor," he said proudly. He patted the pillow next to him. "Sit here for a moment, *mi amor*."

She sat, her knees against one another.

"These gentlemen," said Del Valle, "have come from New York to research the uprising here 50 years ago for a film that they are making."

The threesome exchanged quick, "What the fuck?" glances.

"I know you don't want us to announce this around town," said the old guy. "Carlito told me about the project. Don't worry, we will tell no one unless you want me to help with further contacts."

Junior took a deep breath. Incredible! Isn't there an end to the jackasses he had to deal with on this thing? "Thanks, but we got a list of contacts, and places to visit," he told the old guy.

Chucho and Manny took deep gulps of their drink.

"I just want to let you know that I, we, will do all we can to help you tell the true story of the uprising," said Del Valle. "I am available, as is my wife, to tell our stories, to tell the story of Blanquita, our cousin and our closest, dearest friend, to offer you our stories so that you will see that this idea of ending U.S. colonialism on the island, of seizing independence for Puerto Rico so it could take its rightful place among the nations of the world, this idea will never die. Here is Natasha, my granddaughter. Her father, my one and only son, rebelled against the rebellion and, besides becoming a heart surgeon, has turned against the heart of his family and is now a member of the party that wants statehood. Natasha has returned to her family's ideals, those of my father and his father before him. You see, those ideals live on, even if it skips one generation. It will never die."

Junior nodded. Manny kept drinking. Chucho said, "Wow!"

Junior gave Chucho a dark, dirty look, then asked the girl: "How do you feel about all this?" He just wanted to hear her voice.

Her eyes and hair were dark, like Blanca Canales' in the print on the wall, and she had high cheekbones, full lips, and pale, clear skin. She said softly: "It saddens me, you know, that Papi and Abuelo are no longer, well, close to one another, because of, you know, their differences in politics. But, you see, just by looking at the reality one understands that the United States holds the island for colonial purposes so that its businesses can make more money and its military can have bases, such as on Vieques, and not even need the permission of Puerto Ricans to bomb where people live. Well, shouldn't all people have the right to govern themselves completely, without interference from some other country? Why doesn't the U.S. practice what it preaches to the other countries in the world?"

Chucho kept looking at the girl's lips, licking his own as inside his head he saw her on her knees before him. Junior seemed to pierce into Chucho's fantasy. He wanted to break that fuckin' moron's face and softly kiss the wonderful beauty speaking in a low, honeyed voice.

"We are not against the people of the United States," said the girl, "just against some of the policies of the government, especially when it holds back people who would do much better if they got their complete freedom. If the people are given all the facts about the colony and what the island could achieve under independence . . ."

"Right on, sister!" said Chucho, continuing to lick his lips, then winking around the room.

Manny didn't want to hear any more of this political bullshit. He had several phone calls to make to find out if everything was in place in the *puntos*.

Junior said to Chucho: "Why don't you just shut the hell up and let the young lady finish what she's saying. You're so goddamn ignorant, you have no idea what she's trying to tell you."

"No, it's just . . ." Natasha said.

"My granddaughter has a beautiful mind!" said the old guy.

"Hey, I ain't interruptin'," Chucho insisted.

"Just shut . . .!"

"No problema," said Chucho.

"You're the friggin' problem."

"I didn't mean to . . ." Natasha said.

"What you say makes lots of sense," Junior said.

Natasha smiled warmly. Everything about her seemed intelligent and sweet. Still, he should end this particular session.

"We'll be going to our room now. We haven't much time and we have lots of things to plan out, about . . . the film."

"One more round?" asked the old guy. "Only five dollars for follow-up drinks."

"Maybe later," said Junior. "Let's go, guys."

"We serve dinner in one hour, out on the patio," said the old guy. "My Rosa is a wonderful cook. If you would care to join us, we have a special fixed price for the dinner tonight. We have *mofongo* and we have *sopa de pollo* and we have . . ."

"That sounds real good," said Junior. "We'll be there."

They went to their large, airy room fronted by a balcony. Manny went onto the balcony to make calls on his cell phone about his "business arrangements."

Chucho leaned back on his elbows on one of the beds. "Hey, when are we gonna start shooting the movie?" he said, cackling. "I wanna put that beauty downstairs in a leading role. All she got to do is give me a deep throat blow job and I'll make her a big star."

"Shut up, asshole!" said Junior, who was looking through his overnight bag. "I see you making any move on that girl, I'll cripple you."

"Why? You want her for yourself?"

Junior pulled a black snub-nosed .38 from his bag and aimed it at Chucho's head. Chucho sat up. Junior pulled the trigger and Chucho jumped off the bed. The bullets were in a separate place in the bag.

"*Fuck*, man!"

"Behave yourself," said Junior with a smile. He loaded the gun, then put it into his pants pocket. "We don't wanna leave nothing around the room could get us in trouble," he said as Manny came in from the balcony.

"You leave these guys on their own, they're gonna fuck up everything," said Manny, jerking his head toward the balcony doors, open to the quickly darkening evening. "I hope we can get this shit over with by tomorrow. I got to get back to my business."

"What's this about us making a film?" Junior asked Manny.

Manny shrugged. "That dumbass husband of the woman who got us the school addresses. I don't know, he wanted to make himself look important or something to the old guy, his uncle. Who the fuck knows?"

Manny went back out to the balcony to make some more calls. Chucho went into his overnight bag to get out his own Smith & Wesson Bodyguard snub-nosed .38. He dramatically pointed it in the air and spun the cylinder. He took bullets from the box in his luggage, loaded the cylinder, and spun it again.

"You're right, man, we should be carrying at all times," said Chucho, giving a sneering smile to Junior. He pocketed the pistol and plopped down on the bed again and was soon asleep, snoring through his open mouth.

Junior was tempted to stuff a pair of socks or something into the little motherfucker's pie-hole. Instead, he went out to the balcony, got the list of schools from Manny, came back in and lay back on the other bed (a cot was folded against the wall). He took out the map of Jayuya from the lobby, unfolded it and tried to match the schools with their locations on the map. It wasn't easy. The map showed some outlying barrios without several street names and Junior had to approximate where several of the schools might be. He made marks on the map with his ballpoint, trying to figure how to cover the locations in the shortest time. They only had the one car. If some of the schools were close by they could divide them up and meet at a central point. Next to each school, he wrote who would go to which principal's office and say he was the brother of Richie Pérez, there was an emergency, their mother was very sick, If they found that he was at the school, they would grab him and take him back to San Juan, to Papo's brother-in-law's shed behind the guest house. They would lock him up there until he came up with the money. He would have a very short time if he wanted to go on living with fingers, toes and a face.

Chucho woke with a gasp. He bolted up. "Where the fuck . . .?" He blinked, then announced: "Hey, I'm hungry. When do we eat?"

Junior's stomach was rumbling also. He hadn't had anything since morning coffee and bread. "O.K.," he said, leaving the list on the bed to be finished up later, "it's about an hour. Let's go downstairs."

Dinner was in the patio at the back of the house. Only one of the half dozen or so tables in the patio was occupied. Two aging tourists in safari jackets sat at the table close to the door to the kitchen. The man was bald and goateed and the woman was very thin with a tanned, wrinkled face. She sat a head taller than the guy. The guy smiled at Junior and his companions and the threesome grunted back as they crossed to a table under a large ceiba tree.

Natasha, the granddaughter, came over to take their orders, asking if they would like drinks first. Manny and Chucho ordered Corona beer and Junior asked for a "Puerto Rico Libre."

When the girl brought the drinks, Chucho said: "Hey, a great student, a soon-to-be doctor, a revolutionary and a real beauty of a waitress. I bet you could also be a terrific model. Let me see you walk. Go ahead, swing your hips."

Natasha blushed.

Junior said to Chucho: "Why don't you shut your stupid mouth? Leave her alone, she's working."

Chucho drank from his beer bottle.

After another round of drinks, they ate *mofongo* and had *flan* and coffee. Junior had a Felipe Segundo brandy.

Then the couple from the other occupied table came over. The bald-headed guy said: "We definitely do not want to waste your precious time, but I feel we should meet each other. I am Herman Stoltz and this is my wife, Dagmar. We are professors on leave from the Universitat Leipzig."

The six-foot Dagmar offered the smallest of a thin-lipped smile.

"We are archeo-anthropologists studying the Taíno culture. I'm sure, as well-known American filmmakers, you are aware as to its importance throughout the Caribbean and that this lovely city pays homage to that culture with its museums and petroglyphs—that is, rock carvings.

"As I'm sure you know, and intend to show in your film, this lovely town is located on the skirts of the "Tres Picachos" or Three Peaks mountain, a shape that resembles that of the *cemí*, the fundamental symbol of the Taíno religion with its three cardinal points: *Yocahu, Bagua, Maorocoti.* As I'm sure you know, on top of the sacred mountain peak, in the *turey*—that is, the sky—there resides *Yaya*, the Creator, whose name means that which has neither beginning nor end and which has no male ancestor or creator."

"Good old *Yaya*," said Chucho, who was sucking on a third bottle of beer. "Did people really believe in that shit?"

The bald guy kept smiling. "We are in need of filmmakers of your caliber to document for us several of the artifacts and scenery here, and since Don Rafael has informed us that you are famous filmmakers from the United States, we would like to propose, if you have the time, some film work for us, for which the Archeology Department of the Universitat will pay you well, I believe. Perhaps we could work out some . . ."

Chucho let out a whooping laugh. Junior sliced him with eye daggers. Manny rolled his eyes. "We don't do outside contracts," said Junior.

"Hey, maybe if we get paid first," said Chucho.

"Maybe you should shut up," said Junior.

The tall woman spoke in German to her husband, then switched to English. "Let us go, Herman. I don't believe these people would understand our project." She threw looks around the table that showed she thought the "filmmakers" were ignorant, stupid, and indecent, among other things.

"*Ja*, but . . ."

"Poof!" said the woman, looking down at her husband. She glanced again around the table. "Poof!" she said and walked through the door leading back into the house. Herman followed.

"What the fuck was that all about?" said Chucho.

"Fuckin' Don Rafael blew our cover," said Manny.

"He *provided* us with cover," Junior said, lighting up a cigar he had bought in San Juan. He narrowed his narrow eyes even narrower as he blew out smoke and looked at his two cohorts. He preferred to think of them as minions. He wanted to ditch them soon as this was over. In fact, maybe he would pull out from Papo too when they got back to the city. Maybe he would even go back to school. He was tired of spending all his time with mindless jerkoffs.

Back in the room, Chucho had another attack and spent the next hour in and out of the bathroom. "My stomach is all fucked up," he kept announcing.

Manny took to the balcony to make more phone calls. Junior mapped out their route to the schools around the town. He finished up and feeling restless went downstairs again.

At a makeshift bar in the reception room, Don Rafael poured Junior another Felipe Segundo. He was about to engage Junior in conversation about "the war for independence," but Junior said, "I got to get some air," and took his drink out to the porch.

Sitting on a rocker out there and reading a book was Natasha. She turned down the book on her lap when Junior sat on the rocker next to her. She was smoking a cigarette, which gave Junior a good feeling. She wasn't a health nut. The air was refreshing, almost chilly, a beautiful night in the mountains.

He took another cigar out of the top pocket of his short-sleeved shirt. He was going to ask her if she minded if he lit up a cigar, then told himself: What the hell, she's smoking too.

"I hope Abuelo didn't put you in an uncomfortable position, as far as your film is concerned," Natasha said. "He is very fervent in his beliefs. He's lived through a lot and unlike others who talk a lot, he knows things first-hand."

"No problem. Everyone has what he believes in. You believe what you believe."

"And you—what do you believe in?"

Junior took puffs on his cigar, let out smoke, took a sip of his brandy. Anyone else, he would tell them, none of your fuckin business. But, crazy, he felt he had to explain . . . something . . . in the best way possible to this lovely girl.

"What I believe in is doing what's best for myself and for what's mine. I ain't married no more, my wife died a couple years ago. But I got a big family."

"Oh, I'm so sorry about your wife," said Natasha.

So he killed the bitch off. Being a junkie somewhere in San Juan is the same as being dead.

"Cancer," he said.

All junkies have it, he thought.

"I'm so sorry."

Junior shrugged. "That's life," he said. "What about you? What are you going to be doin'?"

"Well, I start medical school at the University in September. My father became a cardiologist and a heart surgeon. I want to be a neurologist, to study the brain."

Say something intelligent! All he could come up with was, "Terrific!"

"That's a lot more years of study. I got a scholarship for the first year, at least."

"Well, I hope you make it," said Junior. "I'm sure you will."

"Yes," said Natasha, whom Junior realized was no shrinking violet, "I believe I will."

"I think you're something special," said Junior. Why not?

"You don't even know me. Not really." She shook her head. But she seemed pleased.

"Hey, there are things," said Junior, "that someone just knows. I know about you. You're special."

"Well, I have a goal and I'm going to do what I can to reach it. For myself, but for my country too."

Here comes the political bullshit, Junior thought. But he didn't mind listening to it from this girl.

It never came.

Natasha crushed out her cigarette in an ashtray on the wide armrest of the rocker. They looked deeply at one another like they were getting ready for a long, impassioned kiss.

But Natasha said, "I really have to go now. It's been very nice talking to you." She got up and disappeared inside.

Junior took a deep breath, finished his brandy, put out his cigar, then went through the screened door.

Upstairs, the two assholes were snoring away. He got undressed and got under the sheets. It was a nice cool night in the mountains.

What a lovely babe! He'd think of a way to see her again. Maybe something good would come out of this friggin trip.

TWENTY-TWO

Junior woke with the sun and clapped his hands loudly to wake the two jerks, then jiggled their beds to get them on their feet.

"Fuck!" said Chucho. "I was dreamin' I was doing that chick from downstairs."

"Shut up and get dressed!" Junior ordered.

They drove into town and grabbed coffee and Egg McMuffins at a drive-through. They took off, but Chucho had to take a crap again and they drove back to the McDonald's.

"My stomach is all fucked up," Chucho announced for the tenth time.

By one p.m., they had covered the twelve schools on the list, going from barrio-to-barrio, parking across the street while either Junior or Manny went to the principal's office. (Junior told Chucho he couldn't trust him, he might shit in his pants while in the office).

No Richie Pérez at any of the schools.

Fuckin great. thought Junior as he strode from the office of the last listed public grammar school. Girls in their red-and-gray plaid jumpers and boys in white polo shirts and dark pants looked on from the open-air corridors, giggling and waving at him. Junior got ready to get behind the wheel and go back to the guest house, then on to San Juan, when this little kid came running out of the school, calling: "Meester, Meester." He told Junior to come back to the office.

The principal, Señora Robles, who hadn't been available when Junior visited earlier, was sitting at her desk reading a memo. A plump gray-haired woman, she turned her no-nonsense blue eyes up at Junior and said: "One moment."

She read another memo while Junior waited. He felt like a student about to be chewed out for . . something.

The principal's assistant already had told him there was no Señor Pérez at the school. So why had he been asked back?

Señora Robles finished reading, introduced herself and said: "I understand you are looking for a young man who recently began teaching in Jayuya."

Junior nodded.

No one is teaching here by the name of Pérez. There is a Mrs. Pérez over at the Nemesio Canales School, and a Miss Pérez at the Antonio Romero School, but I know of no male teacher with that name in this municipality, where I have worked at schools for the past forty-two years."

Junior took a deep breath, let it out and nodded again. So what the fuck . . .?

"However," said Señora Robles, "there is a school in Barrio Tamarindo, which is run by Sister Margaret. It is not in the public school system, nor is it a bonafide Catholic school, but it is, one might say, an experimental school, which has had great success with several students who have had difficulty within the public school system. Some of the teachers at the school took part in demonstrations on Vieques, to get the Navy to halt its military exercises that are causing many problems. I believe some of them were arrested and remain in jail. I would imagine that substitutes have been brought in to teach. Perhaps the Pérez you are looking for is now teaching there."

"Could you show me how to get to the school?" Junior asked.

Señora Robles called out: "Lo-la!"

The same small skinny girl from the outer office who Junior spoke to earlier came timidly into the principal's office.

"Tell this gentleman how to get to Sister Margaret's school in Barrio Tamarindo."

The girl made a little curtsey and asked Junior to follow her. She led him outside, then pointed to a hill behind where the car was parked. "It is there," she said. "On top of the hill." She made another curtsey and hurried back to the school.

Junior got back into the car. Now all he had to do was find the way up there.

They drove to the end of the street and found a rutted road that led further into the hills. After several minutes of twists and turns, they entered a barrio with a few stores and rickety wooden and boxy, one-story houses. A jíbaro-looking old guy in a straw hat was coming out of a colmado. Junior shouted to him: *"Donde está la escuela?"*

The old guy pointed to a two-story gray concrete building at the end of the street. *"Ahí, ahí,"* he said.

They parked across the road from the school. "I got a strong feeling that our boy is at this school," Junior said, staring at the small Puerto Rican and U.S. flags flying from a second-floor window.

"So let's go the fuck in there and get him," said Chucho.

"So let's shut the fuck up," said Junior, "and use our brains to figure out what we're gonna do."

Chucho got out of the car. "I gotta go to the bathroom," he said. He walked down the street to the colmado, disappeared inside. Minutes later, he came out carrying a six-pack.

"The guy let me use his toilet," he said, handing beer bottles to Junior and Manny.

They drank and waited.

Chucho went for another trip to the bathroom and came back with another six-pack, and they drank that too.

Adults started showing up and kids scampered out of the school. A tall nun peered out the front door. She looked around, noticed the car with a questioning expression, then returned to the school. No Richie Pérez.

Fuck!" said Junior. He let out a deep belch and was about to heave himself out of the car when Richie Pérez appeared at the front door of the school. He held the hand of a little girl of six or seven.

Junior hauled himself back, ducked down and ordered the others to do the same. Richie and the little girl walked down the opposite side of the street. After they were almost out of sight, Junior started up the car and it crept down the road.

"We ain't gonna let that little kid stop us from snatching up that rat, are we?" asked Chucho.

Junior told Chucho: "Shut the fuck up!"

TWENTY-THREE

This is what happened, as far as I know.

I was in the teacher's lounge making coffee through a coffee sock when Sister Margaret came in. She told me that the father of little Luz Figueroa wanted to pick up his daughter at noon, rather than after class. He had gotten a call from a friend working in Ponce. There had been an accident at the condominium they were building and three workers were badly injured. They needed additional workers, and that would mean he would have to go to Ponce right away. He would finally have a job, for a couple of months anyway. Since his wife was working in Ponce as a domestic, he would have to bring Luz over to the house of Doña Francisca, who would watch her until her mother came home.

I told Sister I knew where Doña Francisca lived. She was a night-class student of mine, learning to read and write, and one night during a downpour I had walked her home under the school's umbrella. So the dad didn't have to come; I would walk Luz to Doña Francisca's house after school.

I would drop off Luz, then go to Pucho's colmado to call Prof. Camacho and tell him I appreciated all he had done for me, but I didn't think I needed bodyguards. What would I say at the school when they found out about the bodyguards, which I'm sure would happen in this small barrio. That I'm a drug dealer on the run from other drug dealers?

To be honest, I was down on myself, and on lots of other things. Julia, who wasn't all that smart or sweet, wanted me to move in with her, which was about the last thing I wanted to do. The kids at the school were terrific, but the longer I stayed there, the longer I wouldn't be doing anything to set up the scholarship in Laura's name. And what good would be anything if I couldn't do something for Laura's memory? So I was in pretty much of a funk and my feelings were, let what happens, happen.

I left Luz with Doña Francisca, then, since I lived just down the road, I decided to go home for a quick shower and sandwich. I took change I had in a coffee can for the phone call to the prof. When I came out of the house, I saw a car parked across the road. I had noticed the same car parked across from the school but didn't think anything about it then. The driver called me over.

He knew my name!

I turned, to look at Junior, Papo's guy in New York.

"Come here," he said, "I wanna talk to you."

Manny El Bronx and that other one from New York, that little snake, Chucho, were sitting in the back.

Chucho said: "Get the fuck in the car." The back door opened. I froze.

First, I should give a layout of the location of my shack. It was in a wooded area. There were just a few other houses down this particular road, each spaced about 100 feet from the other. The woods ran about 50 feet back before they sloped steeply down the side of a mountain.

"Get the fuck in!" Junior repeated. I still didn't move.

Chucho jumped out of the back of the car. "Get in, asshole!" He held a pistol in his hand. I looked at him like he was talking in a foreign language.

Chucho pointed the gun at my head. His eyes got tight. Then he whipped the pistol up and fired one, then two, shots in the air.

"What the fuck . . .? Idiot!" Junior looked at Chucho like he should be locked in a Hannibal Lecter straightjacket.

They came out of the woods, from behind my house, crouched over with short-barreled rifles. They were dressed in camouflage fatigues. I just caught a glimpse of them before Chucho pocketed his pistol, took out his switchblade, sliced a couple of buttons off my shirt and pushed me into the back of the car, then got in himself.

They came around each side of the car. One of them shoved his rifle into Junior's face. "Show me your hands!" he shouted. Fully standing, he was about six-foot, five-inches. "Get out of the car. Everybody, out!"

"You're all under arrest," said the other guy.

"Who the fuck are you?" asked Junior.

"None of your fuckin business," said the guy with the rifle still in Junior's face. "One of you pulled a gun on an innocent citizen, shots were fired, we heard you threaten to take him away against his will. Your police records will be checked. I'm making a citizen's arrest."

The other rifleman was on a walkie-talkie, speaking in police code: "It's a two-zero-seven Alpha."

The tall guy told Papo's three goons to put their hands against the car, lean forward and spread their legs. Each had a pistol and Chucho and Manny had knives. About fifteen minutes later, a whole bunch of police cars pulled up with uniformed cops who handcuffed Junior and the others and put each of them in the back seat of a patrol car and sped away.

So that was it. No drama, no shootouts, except for Chucho's crazy shots in the air.

Except that wasn't the end of it.

The riflemen told me they were from Betancourt Security in San Juan, sent to give me close protection. They had arrived barely half an hour earlier and were setting up a security tent behind my house before contacting me about how they would provide my protection. They planned to stay out of sight, close to the school and to my house, assuring me I could go about my life normally, but I would be under constant close vigilance.

All of which no longer was necessary, right? I said.

Probably not, they answered. They would contact the San Juan office.

"Thanks," I said. What else could I say?

"That's what we do," said the really tall guy.

I went to Pucho's and called professor Camacho and told him what happened. I thanked him also for probably saving my life (I definitely would not have emptied my bank account of the scholarship money to give to Papo and his goons), not mentioning that I hadn't agreed to the protection, so why did he send it? I guess he just took it on himself, whether I would have agreed to it or not. Like he was taking control of my life. My safety, anyway. I guess I should have been grateful. Which I was. But not completely.

The next day, Sister Margaret told me that the appeals court in Boston had reduced the prison terms of the nuns and the other demonstrators to time already served. Money had been raised to pay all the fines. The regular school term was ending in two weeks, but there would be a summer school and, if I wanted, I could stay on and teach. I asked Sister Margaret if I could give her an answer in a couple of days. She agreed.

The day after that, Professor Camacho told me that Junior and his friends were brought to a jail in San Juan, charged with attempted kidnapping and violating the Weapons Law. The judge put this real high bond on their release so they wouldn't cut out for the States. Then they were indicted by a Grand Jury since it was a federal case because they came down from the States to Puerto Rico to do the kidnapping. They were being held awaiting trial. Since I was the victim, the prof said, I would have to testify. That would blow my cover, or whatever I got between me and what I was sure would be heavy prison time.

So "the game," or whatever the fuck it was, was up. My fate twisted through my stomach.

I had to stay together at least until the term was over. Then I would end my brief teaching career and go back to San Juan and decide what to do next.

The night before I left for San Juan, I asked Julia to my shack. "The school term is over and I'm going back to San Juan and maybe leaving the island," I told her.

"You are leaving me?"

"No, I mean, yeah. No, I'm not leaving *you*, I'm just leaving my situation here because . . . well, because . . . I need to do other things now."

"What things?" She seemed more curious than angry.

What was I going to tell her? That too many times she was too harsh, too humorless, too serious for me? That I wanted to get out of something I should never have gotten into in the first place? That I lacked the . . . what? . . . the daring, the bravado, the guts to find ways to soften her harshness, her despair?

So all I could say was that I was sorry. I went to kiss her, but she pushed me away, then slapped my face, then broke into tears. Then she left.

To be honest, I would say that I wasn't mature enough to work toward developing a lasting relationship. I wanted to feel deep love right away. That's what happened between Laura and me.

I didn't want the responsibilities of only receiving while I found a way to give what was not yet in my heart. I wasn't mature enough for that.

But at least I did realize that it was time to grow up.

TWENTY-FOUR

My first stop after leaving Barrio Tamarindo was to visit my mom. I spent a weekend eating up a storm and being put under the third-degree.

Why had I taken the teaching job in the mountains? What about my classes at the University? Why was it still so difficult to get in touch with me? Where was I going now? What was going to become of me?

I told her the best half-truths I could come up with: I had misplaced my cell phone; I decided to take the teaching job because I was getting tired of just going to classes and studying all the time. This was a great opportunity to work out on the island. My professors understood and I could make up the incompletes in summer school. I was going back to San Juan and would start the summer classes very soon. Bye, Mom. Thanks for the great meals, no one makes *pasteles* like you. I'll call in a couple of days to give you the number of my new cell phone.

"What am I going to do with you?"

What you have learned to do, for which I'm grateful: let me live my own life while bugging me just a couple of times a week.

"What's going to become of you?"

That's a tough one. "Everything will be fine. Don't worry, Mom. What'll be, 'll be."

"*No, mi hijo*. What will be is what you work towards making it."

Where's that Puerto Rican fatalism? I guess living in the States made her lose it. I, of course, didn't say anything yet, but I'd decided on my next move while I was in a crowded *público* going to Arecibo. It came to me as the right thing and really the only thing to do. I was sure this decision would break Mom's heart. But maybe she'll understand. Maybe others will also. Maybe.

Back in Río Piedras, Mike Padilla broke the news to me. After I knocked on the door, he came out into the hallway rather than asking me in. "Our" room no longer was mine.

"No one knew when you would be coming back, or if," said Mike. "So my buddy Octavio Torres, who's also in the law school, he was looking for a place, since he broke up with his girlfriend and . . . well, he moved in a few days ago, and he's still getting his stuff together and . . ."

I couldn't blame Mike. He was worried about the rent.

"So where's my books and the baseball stuff I didn't take?"

"It's all still here. We just put everything in the closet. You wanna come in and pick it all up now?"

"No, I'll get it later. Just take care of it for a while longer, O.K.?"

"Yeah, sure."

Mike seemed relieved that I wasn't blaming him for renting out my part of the room. I was pretty sure that Señora Súarez was putting the pressure on for him to get another paying roommate.

Then Mike asked me: "How's your Mom?"

"Fine," I said. "I just came from visiting her. Why you asking?"

"Wow, I'm glad to hear that. The reason is that this guy called me some days ago to ask how he could get in touch with you. He said you weren't answering your cell and he had to speak to you, it was important. He said your Mom was very sick and she gave him your number, but you weren't answering, so she gave him my number. She was really sick and couldn't talk, so I gave him the number that Señora Súarez gave me."

"Yeah, I called Señora Súarez when I was in New York asking her to get a message to you about calling me. I wanted to borrow some money to get a plane ticket back. Well, I made the arrangements another way."

Mike flushed. "I was gonna call you back, right away, but I was really busy, so I decided I would do it the next day. Then the guy called for your number. So I gave it to him. I called the next day, and several times after, but there was no answer."

At least that solved the mystery of how Chucho called me while I had Tony's cell phone. He got Mike's number from my cell, then called me after Mike gave him Tony's number, which he got from Señora Súarez.

"Was it O.K. that I gave the number?" Mike looked guilty. "He said your Mom . . . I was gonna call right away but I had this class . . ."

What the fuck was I going to say. Mike was . . . Mike.

"Yeah," I said, "No problem."

We shook hands, rather than embraced. "See you around," I said.

"Sure, I'll see you on campus," Mike said.

"Yeah, sure," I said with a smile.

My next stop was at the University, to see Professor Camacho. I wanted to tell him about my decision. When I found him coming out of a class, I invited him and his wife to dinner to thank them for their help, and to discuss with them my future plans. The prof said I should come over to their house for dinner, but I insisted on taking them out and we set it up for the end of the week.

So here I was, homeless again. I hated to do it but I went into the scholarship account another time for my living expenses and rented a cheap room in a rooming house on Plaza de Armas. I spent the next few days convincing myself that what I decided was the right thing to do. Actually, it was the only thing to do. Forget right or wrong, good or bad. It was what I had to do to keep living with myself. I finally realized what I did, among other things, was to help these guys carry out their slimy business. This doesn't mean I'm going to give up on the scholarship. I'll get the money other, better, ways, no matter how long it takes.

I met the Camachos in Sam's Patio, at a table in the back. We ordered, then I got right to it. "I'm gonna turn myself in."

Ralph and Tere looked at each other, as though each was checking what they heard. Then Ralph turned to me. He stared at me with a sort-of inquisitive, sort-of pitying, sort-of skeptical smile.

"It's what I have to do," I said. "I'm going to tell them about the times I took the drugs to New York. If they ask, which I'm sure they will, then I'll tell them who gave me the drugs here and who I delivered them to up there."

The prof looked at his wife again. She gave a little nod like she confirmed they were hearing the same thing.

"So I wanted to tell you, and"—looking over at Mrs. Camacho—"I thought you could tell me just what I had to do, who I should see."

"Are you sure you want to do that?" Tere Camacho asked. "You know, once the transportation of drugs across state lines is involved, this becomes a case for the federal court. And once that happens, the judge has to follow certain strict sentencing guidelines."

"Yeah, I expect to go to prison."

She put her hands out, palms up, as though expecting a further explanation. All I could do was shrug.

Mrs. Camacho looked at me unsmiling, going from my eyes to around my face and back to my eyes. She was looking for an answer to her next question. "Why are you doing this?"

I shrugged. What could I tell her? "I just know I have to."

Another long pause. There were more long looks between the prof and his wife.

"I was wondering whether Legal Services could take my case. And whether you could be my lawyer."

"I'm not a criminal attorney," said Mrs. Camacho. She took a long sip of her beer. Then she took a very deep breath. "I suppose I could get one of the other attorneys to work with me on this."

"If you could, that would be great. I don't know how to thank you."

"The dinner will do for now." She finally smiled.

"Yeah, but . . ."

"Just finish your hamburger," said my attorney.

All that followed was not quite as planned. As if life could be planned, even in the broadest outline.

Well, maybe.

No, not really.

I went to see a federal attorney, accompanied by Mrs. Camacho. I signed something called a proffer letter, then I spilled the beans on my contacts, meaning Manny El Bronx, Junior, Chucho, and Papo. The hell with them. They were out to screw me, so I didn't mind screwing them. I was really looking forward to turning state's evidence against Manny El Bronx. The sonovabitch set me up, I couldn't be happier to bring him down. Chucho was a rotten little asshole and Junior, who seemed to have some brains, should have known better than to blame me for the drug shortage. I said I didn't mind going to prison. The Assistant U.S, Attorney, a guy with pale blue eyes behind rimless glasses, raised his long, pale face from something he was writing, and lifted a long, thin, blond eyebrow at me. Tere Camacho looked at me and frowned.

The Assistant U.S. Attorney asked me about my trips and the payment I got for each trip. He didn't ask where the money was and didn't say anything about my having to return it. But I couldn't help thinking that I really shouldn't be keeping this money. So that evening I wrote out a check for the $14,402 in the bank to Hogar CREA, which works with addicts to get them off drugs. Like I said, there was no right or wrong, as far as my decisions about my drug-running days were concerned. All I knew was I no longer wanted that money for the scholarship or for anything else. After I got out of prison, I would work long and hard and save almost everything for the scholarship in Laura's name.

The Assistant U.S. Attorney told me what I told him would be used in a further indictment of my "buddies," this time on drug conspiracy charges to accompany the attempted kidnapping. And the proffer letter meant that more or less I had immunity! That's if I was telling the truth.

So was I off the prison hook? Maybe. Maybe not.

I got a tiny apartment on Sol Street in Old San Juan and a job as a bartender-waiter in a restaurant across from the old post office-courthouse. I spent my free hours reading—Professor Camacho lent me books by Conrad, et al—and I tried to write every day. What was I writing? Whatever came into my head: memories, notes on my feelings about things, a couple of short stories. I visited the prof and his wife-my attorney at least once a week. They insisted I come over for dinner every Monday, my evening off.

Then, Eva came back into my life.

"Here is the book about a love that survives half a century, perhaps longer, perhaps forever, despite the vagaries of life," she wrote in a note accompanying the copy of *Love in the Time of Cholera*. (She got my new address from Tony, who I kept in touch with by e-mail.) "I just love this book about the realities and un-realities of love and I hope you love it too."

I wrote her a letter, telling her I was looking forward to reading it, adding that I supposed I had to settle at this point for vicarious love. She actually wrote a pen-on-stationary letter back. It included her thoughts on love, via Keats, who, she noted, had written: "I am certain of nothing but the holiness of the heart's affections, and the truth of imagination."

Sounded good to me. So I answered. Pen on paper. And she answered same.

I didn't tell her, but I didn't intend to read the García Márquez book just yet. I'd wait until after I finished Conrad and Melville and a few other sea sagas.

She sent me some of her poems, "Your poetry," I wrote, "shows me that you understand the heart's long journey and what it searches for."

I included a short story in the next letter.

"You really captured the psyche of that woman in your story about the isolated community," wrote Eva. "We see her needs, her stubbornness while intimating the stored-up love in her soul that is waiting for, *wanting* release."

I told her about the upcoming trial and said when it was over I wanted to see her and Tony, I'd come up to New York. She said that would be great, but greater still would be if she could also visit me in "our beautiful Puerto Rico."

Once more, I felt a flush of guilt at my happiness and anger at my guilt and further guilt at my anger. Then I ordered myself to stop the stupidity. I knew there would always be an unhealed wound in my heart that no one would be able to reach. But I decided that, in time, I did want a deeper relationship with Eva.

"By all and every means possible, come for a visit," I replied.

Then, three months later, in September, the trial against Manny El Bronx and the New York hoods began.

TWENTY-FIVE

Here's how the trial went down: Felix Fuentes, attorney to the island drug czars and lesser dealers, said the defendants were just trying to resume an old friendship they had with me when I had lived in New York. He told the jury that they were being given the opportunity to right a grievous wrong by acquitting his clients of all the charges brought against them.

Pacing in front of the table where Junior, Chucho and Manny El Bronx sat in their orange prison suits, Fuentes told the jury: "These young men, the defendants in this trumped-up case against them, these three fellows are guilty of nothing more than trying to resume an old friendship with a *pana,* a buddy, from the old neighborhood. The two young men from New York, who returned with great joy to *la isla,* their true homeland, on a much anticipated vacation, and who, while here, met up with a third friend who knew the whereabouts of"—Fuentes looked down at the sheet of paper on the table in front of him—"of Steven Pérez, who was residing in the bucolic mountain town of Jayuya. They decided to visit their old friend in his new home outside of the hustle and bustle of San Juan." The lawyer made it sound like I was living the easy life in some sort of country mansion.

"The visit was to be a surprise. And a surprise it certainly was, for these fellows when Mr. Pérez accused them of trying to 'kidnap'— the attorney made quote marks with his fingers—yes, *kidnap* him. May I add, in no way were drugs involved in their visit."

Then Fuentes turned to the table. A guard stood behind each of the defendants. Fuentes went to Manny El Bronx, extended his hand. They shook hands. "Good day, Manuel," he said. "Not to worry, your 17-month-old son. Manuel Jr., is receiving the best of care since he was taken from you by the Social Services Department. That's what I've been assured, anyway."

Fuentes wheeled around to again address the jury. "Manuel Rivera, who has worked at odd jobs on the island, and whose wife had died not too long ago because of the incompetent ambulance service connected to our public hospitals, is a young widower trying to raise the infant son." Fuentes pushed a thumb over his shoulder toward Manny El Bronx without turning to look at him. "This, ladies and gentlemen of the jury, is an eager-to-succeed young man who through savings from odd jobs intends to put himself through night school to earn a business degree once he is set free to reunite with his son."

He continued, his usually strong voice now lowered and somewhat shaky, "Manuel Rivera has known little more than grief and sadness in his less than thirty years on this Earth. He was born into poverty in a South Bronx tenement, many of whose occupants were addicted to drugs. Returning to his ancestral home, he found a young woman with whom he thought he could build a better life, a close-knit family life, after the birth of their son, Manuel Jr. But just a year ago, he lost his beloved wife, who suffered a heart attack, most likely brought on from overwork from her waitressing jobs, as well as her tasks as a devoted mother and homemaker. The unfortunate young woman was born with a heart condition. She tragically died before her husband's very eyes, as they waited for the ambulance that never arrived while she still lived.

"But this young man has not given up hope. He continues the struggle—a struggle, I should add, which he has assured me would never cease—to give his loving son a life worthy of the sacrifice of the boy's young, beloved mother."

The attorney's deep brown eyes were actually tear-rimmed. His well-tanned bald head shone under the neon lights in the windowless federal courtroom.

Fuentes said little, if anything, about Junior and Chucho. Each had a record in New York and had spent time on Rikers Island, according to the Assistant U.S. Attorney. Fuentes was trying to appeal to the local jury with the hope that the two Nuyoricans would be carried along in a favorable verdict.

The two private security guards testified on the kidnapping charges, and so did I, as well as giving a play-by-play of my drug mule days in connection with the three guys on trial. The Assistant U.S. Attorney showed evidence of my drug-delivery travels with air receipts, including my tickets bought by one Manuel Rivera, alias Manny El Bronx. I related the dispute over the supposed drug shortage on my last trip and the earlier kidnapping. The Assistant U.S. Attorney presented further airline and hotel records as evidence of my days as a drug mule.

Then Fuentes cross-examined me.

"Now, young man," he said with a quivering smile that meant that whatever I would say would be bullshit, "are we really telling the truth, the whole truth, and nothing but the truth, or have we fabricated this story for our own selfish ends?"

What the hell was he talking about?

"Do you, or I should say, did you know Laura Rosario?"

"I told you I did. I told you what happened to her at the University and why I started delivering drugs. So I could start a scholarship for . . ."

"Yes, yes. But what did you *not* tell us?" Fuentes' eyes looked ready to pop out of his head.

"I don't know what you're talking about."

"You don't know?" He gave me, the judge, the jury, a startled, snarky smile. "May I propose young man, that you may never have had the noble motives you claim for becoming an integral part of the illegal drug trade between the island and the States. The fact is that there was no engagement, no announcement of an impending marriage, nothing but your word that you began to deliver drugs out of love for this unfortunate young lady, rather than for the one and only real reason that anyone goes into the narcotics trade: self-enrichment."

Fuentes slowly shook his head, as though really disappointed at me for trying to contradict that indisputable fact. Then looking at me, but addressing everyone else, especially the judge and the jury, he said:

"I have one crucial question: Why should your testimony— you, who admittedly was in the business of bringing illegal narcotics from the island to the States for profit—why should your testimony be trusted over, for instance, the young widower on trial who was trying to raise a son, to give the boy a secure place in this often insecure world? Why should you be believed over a young father?

"Take, for instance, the flight ticket paid for by Mr. Rivera for Mr. Steven Pérez. With all due respect to the U.S. Attorney's office, it may be that it had no knowledge of the fact that the two young men actually were close friends from their days in the Bronx and

Mr. Rivera has testified that the ticket was bought as a belated birthday present. Perhaps," he said, stroking his dimpled, jutting jaw, "perhaps he who has been the instigator of this case should really be the one facing charges."

"Objection," said the Assistant U.S. Attorney. The judge nodded.

That friggin Fuentes was trying to portray me as a drug-dealing liar who for some weird reason, known only to myself, was trying to incriminate three former buddies from the old neighborhood. He was telling the feds that I had duped them and that they should be bringing charges against me.

The bullshit went on and on, it was pretty pathetic. But the jury was in no rush. They adjourned the first day without coming to a verdict.

What the fuck? If these guys were found not guilty, would that mean I had implicitly been found guilty of somehow setting this whole thing up? Would I then be prosecuted for *my* drug activities, and maybe perjury, and who the hell knew what else?

But it turned out that maybe the jury only wanted another night at a hotel and another free dinner. Because early the next morning, they came back with a verdict. All three were found guilty of drug law violations, attempted kidnapping and illegally carrying weapons. I was later assured by the Assistant U.S. Attorney that I would not be prosecuted. I was home free. Sort of.

The trial had been covered by the island press and the coverage grew as people got really interested when the riot at the University against the Navy and the death of Laura were brought up again. I was even mentioned in an editorial in the local newspaper that supported independence for the island.. "The young woman who tragically lost her life was not only the victim of the stray bullet that killed her on that terrible day at the University. She also was the latest victim of a more than one-hundred-year-old colonial relationship that allows the colonizer to treat the colonized as it will. One could also make the argument that even the young man who became a drug mule was another victim . . ."

Which is not the way I see myself. Anyway, the upshot of the new focus on Laura was that an island fundraiser was held over television. For 24 hours, entertainers, politicians, ballplayers, beauty queens, union chiefs, heads of various civic organizations, barrio organizers, even two bank presidents appeared—all pledging enough to get the Laura Rosario Scholarship for the Study of

Hispanic Literature off the ground at the University of Puerto Rico and flying high for years to come.

Chucho looked for a reduced sentence by squealing on Papo as the head of their New York operations. Manny El Bronx did the same to his suppliers in Puerto Rico. Junior got fifteen years, his onetime buddies ten years each.

A couple of weeks after he was sent to the Atlanta federal penitentiary, Chucho was stabbed to death in the shower. Manny El Bronx, who was in the federal holding pen on the island waiting to be transferred to the States, got both his legs broken.

So far, I was still in one piece.

TWENTY-SIX

Tere Camacho said we should talk to the U.S. Attorney about getting me into a witness protection program. I didn't want that. What the hell, I testified against three guys who were sent to prison. Case closed. That's what I thought. Chucho was knocked off in prison after turning state's evidence against Papo, who I had mentioned in my testimony, and Manny El Bronx was crippled after giving the feds the names of the guys who were the next step up the ladder on the island. So should I be worried? Yes, said Tere Camacho. Better to be safe. So what would I do—live in a safe house with guys with rifles surrounding me whenever I went out, move to Dubuque with a new name? No thanks. I didn't want any protection because I was developing plans of my own.

I didn't relate it before because I didn't want to break up the courtroom action, but on the day I testified, my Mom was sitting in the first row of the spectators' seats, giving the evil eye to Felix Fuentes, the defendants' attorney. Mom had caught the first bus from Arecibo after reading in the newspapers that her son would testify in a federal court drug trial that was somehow going to be tied to the death of a female student during last year's demonstration at the University against the Navy's bombing of Vieques.

After my testimony and the night before the verdict, Mom and I had dinner at the Caribe Hilton. People at the Arecibo City Hall got her a heavily discounted room there.

"What made you do such an insane thing, delivering drugs for those . . . those lowlifes?"

"I did what I had to do, Mom."

"What does that mean—what you *had* to do? What you *had* to do, what you *always have* to do in this life, is use your brains. I didn't see any evidence of this."

A long pause.

Then she said: "Look, *mi'jo*, we've been through a lot together. For so many years we only had each other. Why couldn't you at least have talked to me about what you were planning to do? I could have made suggestions. What kind of son . . .?"

My head started to lighten and my face flush. "Because this was my decision, O.K.? It had nothing to do with you. With you as my mom and me as your son. With anything other than that only I could, and should, make this decision, and I didn't want anyone else influencing me."

Another long pause. With her fork, Mom separated some bones from the red snapper she was eating. She took a deep breath, then looked very deeply into my eyes. "O.K., you did what you did."

She sounded hurt. I should have known that for Mom the moral judgment of my action, so long as I didn't kill or maim anyone, was nowhere as important as whether she knew what was up with me.

Time for a truce. "I'm really sorry I didn't let you know what was going on."

"I'll bet."

I told her I loved her. I asked for her blessing.

"I'd rather slap your face." Another deep sigh, then: *"Que Dios te bendiga."*

After several weeks of exchanging letters, Eva came down to Puerto Rico for a long, four-day weekend with a girlfriend, Michelle. They stayed at a guest house in Ocean Park. After the first night, Eva slept at my apartment. Those dark, dark eyes, those soft lips, that tall, thin, yet full body. A mind that "sees" everything around and inside and even upside down, and puts it all together, what it means and should mean and will mean. She expresses what and why she feels in just the right, beautiful terms, whether writing, poetry or just speaking. I think I may be a taker, but Eva is definitely a giver—of her time, her body, her mind, her sweetest and most challenging thoughts, and all material things. So I fell hard, and I believe she did too.

The plan was that I would come back to New York and while Eva was starting at Hunter College, I would get another teaching job, somewhere in Long Island, if possible. People from the New York schools had been down to the island looking to recruit bilingual teachers, so I shouldn't have a problem. I didn't get to take summer courses for my master's, but I was sure my bachelor's degree would be enough to start a job teaching Latino kids the basics. No one, except Eva, would know my whereabouts, or what I was doing. I would tell my Mom that I was going to California for a year of graduate work at Stanford. I'd keep in touch with her by cell phone. I would keep in touch with the Camachos by e-mail. Besides her academic scholarships, Eva would get a part-time job to earn some money for the family, and since I no longer had to save for the Laura Rosario Scholarship, I'd contribute to Eva's expenses. She would have to tell her mother she was working on the weekends into the early morning hours when I would bring her home in the car I was going to buy. We would spend almost all the weekends in each other's arms.

That was the plan. Here's something beautiful:

When I told Eva all about what I did trying to get money for the scholarship, she said she understood my feelings for Laura, for her memory, what she stood for in Puerto Rico, especially for the students and those who want a better deal for the island. "Maybe both of us can find still another way to keep her memory alive," she said.

A couple of days later she went to a sculptor friend and asked her to make a bust of Laura from a photo. The sculptor agreed. She didn't want anything for the work. Eva said when it's finished we should donate the work to the University if they agree to put it on display. If not, we'd find another public space.

I was all set to gets things going, to fill out applications for teachers' jobs. On my days off from the bar-restaurant, I started a second job, driving tourists around the island for a tour company. I was saving enough to get off to a good start in the states.

But once more the best-laid plans got all fouled up. I should have known. I thought I had put the whole drug business behind me.

I should have known.

After we closed up the bar-restaurant at about one a.m., I would walk Señora Campos to her apartment. She managed the place for a rich relative in Florida. Before closing, she would count the cash and lock it in the office safe. Señora Campos was a widow, in her late sixties, a small, skinny, incredibly spry woman. Even after a night of seating people, collecting money by the cash register, checking on the kitchen and helping mix drinks behind the bar, she was still full of energy. We'd briskly climb the steep hills to Calle Norzagaray, the uppermost street in the Old City, then she'd kiss me on the cheek and enter the mustard-colored building across from Fort San Cristobal, I lived just a couple of blocks away. She always gave her "private bodyguard" extra desserts to take home.

I had just left Señora Campos and was going up Norzagaray, looking forward to eating the *tres leches* I was carrying. When I approached the corner to turn toward my house, a car whizzed by. I heard a pop, which sent me jumping into the shadow of the buildings. I heard another pop. It sounded like two tires had gone flat, yet the car sped up, then screeched and began to make a U-turn in front of the fort.

Those exploding sounds weren't tires going flat. They were two gunshots. Aimed in my direction!

The black Ford started back toward me, then pulled over and jumped the sidewalk. Two guys got out and I dashed across the street where the Old City Wall ran above La Perla. I rushed down steps that led into the barrio.

I looked back. The guys were peering over the wall. Then they started down the steps and I thought of ducking under the railing and getting lost between the houses that sloped down the hill, but I continued to the main street of the slum, which was still alive with loud salsa sounds coming from the open-door bars. Tough-looking characters were leaning against walls of the buildings drinking beer and, I'm sure, selling drugs.

Then I saw the blood. Where the fuck was it coming from?

From the soaked right leg of my khaki pants. From somewhere around the shin, which all of a sudden hurt like hell. I limped and hopped on my left leg as far down the street as I could before I collapsed and dragged myself into an alley. The two guys were about forty yards down on the main street. A couple of other guys from a bar came up to them. My assailants shook their heads and the others kept talking and rotating their hands and my assailants waved pistols over their heads and the guys from the bar split off, walking really fast in different directions.

I pulled up my pants leg. What a bloody mess! One of the bullets must have hit or grazed my leg. I wiped the blood and some of my skin off with the blue bandana I used as a handkerchief, then tied the bandana around the wound, which made my leg hurt even more.

The guys were coming down the street looking between the buildings. I pulled myself up tight against a wall and dragged my right leg down the alley. I was on a small cross street; then I struggled down some concrete steps between one-story cement and wood homes. Dogs were barking and in tiny backyards roosters and chickens were sleeping or still strutting around.

Were the gunmen behind me? I had to get . . . somewhere.

I kept moving as best I could down broken steps and winding paths wide enough for one slender-hipped person. I could hear the boom of the ocean below. A cat brushed by and I jumped away and my right leg gave out and I collapsed on the ground, I pulled myself up and through seemingly impossible slits between one-room shacks.

Then I saw the ocean, the foam leaping and spitting off rocks on a trash-covered beach. A mist was over the water. like a bunch of floating ghosts. A row of tiny shacks stood on crooked stilts behind the beach.

I limped-dragged my body under one of the houses, sat with my legs out in front of me, pulled the injured one up, then slowly slid it down again. The leg shook and the pain was incredible. Leaning my back against a wooden pole, I was breathing heavy, listening to the booming ocean, watching the waves break and crawl almost to where I was. I was sitting on the muddy, trash-filled sand underneath the house, next to beer cans, fast food bags, crushed cigarette packs, flies, mosquitoes, condoms.

Fuck it, I told myself, if they find me, they find me.

The breeze got stronger, and the waves crashed closer on the shore. The water crept up to the edge of the houses. I don't know how I managed, but I still held the box with the cake. I opened the box and started wolfing down the *tres leches*, but it even hurt to friggin swallow.

Then I heard my assailants shouting to each other as they came into view on the beach. Each carried a flashlight and the beams bounced on and under the houses. There was a ripped up, thin mattress under the house where I was hiding and, with great effort and more pain, I turned my body onto my stomach and dragged the mattress over me. I peered from under there and saw the lights still dancing around.

Then I heard them cursing, and they disappeared back up into La Perla.

What I heard next twisted my stomach and loosened my bowels even more. It was coming from under the other houses nearby and it got closer and louder, the shrieking and screeching sound like a stampede of wild animals.

That's just what it was.

They were honking and squealing and dashing from house to house. While there were a couple of small piglets, four or five others were huge, slick and wet, looking as big as rhinos. Seeing me rise from under the mattress, they gave off extra loud squeals and took off down the beach.

Now the waves were breaking at the edges of the houses and water was rushing under them. I was in a goddamn lake.

The next wind gust sounded like a shotgun blast. The ocean flew up to the doors of houses; it crashed and poured under the houses. I struggled back onto the beach and followed the pigs.

I waded along the beach, then pulled myself up some rocks, banging the wound on my leg. I felt like letting go and rolling into the ocean and drowning, but I made it onto a green field about fifty yards across, just outside the fort under the city wall. If the gunmen were nearby, or on top by the wall, they could have picked me off easily.

They weren't there. I dragged myself across the field and up another flight of stone steps to the street above. The black Ford was still parked half in the street and half on the sidewalk.

The wind was clacking the fronds of the palms near the fort. I crossed the field in a downpour and dragged myself down toward Plaza Colón, where I hoped to find a taxi to take me to the hospital.

I made it to Calle San Francisco, to the corner across from the plaza, when both legs gave out and I collapsed by a storefront. The taxi stand was way on the other side of the plaza. A balcony overhanging the store protected me from most of the downpour. I couldn't lift any part of my body. I was fuckin paralyzed. A couple of pedestrians rushing by in the storm looked down at me and kept going.

I was finally able to lift my upper body which I leaned against the chained-up door. I searched my pants pockets. Stupid me. I had made a last minute change of pants before going to work and left my cell phone in my jeans. I was ready to conk out, except the leg wouldn't let me. It was actually jumping around! Or maybe it wasn't. But it felt like it was doing things—raw, skin-scraping, bone-twisting, nerve-tightening things. I pulled up my pants leg. The bandana had rolled down to my ankle and I saw the bloody mess just below my knee and I felt faint again.

Then the three "locas" came dancing by, screaming and laughing as they ducked under the long balcony to get out of the pouring rain. These guy-girls were wearing see-through blouses stuck to their skin by the rain and culottes and platform shoes and each carried a large straw bag. They spotted me, stopped squealing, and asked me how I was. They looked at my leg, issued *"Dios mio"*s, then covered their mouths with their hands. One of them pulled a cell phone from a back pocket and called 911 for an ambulance. Another one pulled a dress and a sweater from a straw bag bunched them together and put the makeshift pillow between my head and the glass door. Then one of them pulled out a pack of cigarettes and I joined the others in a smoke, my first in years, not counting the occasional joint.

We waited for the ambulance. These gay guys didn't know what to do for me, asking if I wanted to call anyone on their cell phones, helping me prop my sagging body up, rearranging the pillow, offering me a sandwich one of them had in his straw bag.

As I declined the sandwich, my head suddenly went light and my eyes closed. When I opened them the three gays were gone.

Standing over me were the two gunmen.

Each looked about seven-foot-tall and they leaned over, whispering something to each other, or to me, then aimed their pistols at my head. They smiled at one another like they were about to join once again in a ritual that gave them great pleasure. I tried to yell, but no sound came. Something was stuck deep in my throat. I couldn't swallow. I couldn't breathe!

My eyes weren't really open, thank God. For a couple of seconds, I went . . . somewhere.

When I opened my eyes for real, the transvestites were still there, fussing over me. One of them was propping me up again. "You got unconscious," he said.

The ambulance finally arrived. I was carried on a stretcher into the back. "You gonna be O.K.," said one of the guys. *"Dios te bendiga,"* said another.

"Thanks," I told them. "God bless you too."

I was taken to the government hospital in a suburb of San Juan. The emergency room was packed. I wasn't the only gunshot victim that night. A shootout between drug gangs had occurred at a nearby housing project and victims were being rolled in on stretchers and wheelchairs, or limping and staggering in on their own or with the help of others.

The medics finally got around to me, giving me a shot to ease the pain. Then, sometime in the middle of the night, pieces of a bullet were dug out and the wound sewed up. My shinbone, or tibia, was smashed and no one knew how I had been able to move around before collapsing on the street. The shooting was reported to the police, one of many that night.

At sunrise, with my right leg bandaged from the knee down and with a pair of crutches under my arms, I was one more barely walking wounded released from the overcrowded hospital.

I phoned the Camachos. The prof drove out to pick me up. He took me to their home. Mrs. Camacho, my lawyer, was saddened and helped put me to bed, but she also was pissed. "I told you," she said, "you can't fool around with these . . . people."

She spoke with the Assistant U.S. Attorney and Professor Camacho spoke with his protection agency friend. While I recuperated at their apartment, I had around-the-clock security, outside the building and around the neighborhood.

The prof said he would make further arrangements with old friends and associates and I said O.K. When I was well enough I did what he had arranged. It meant I had to put off seeing Eva. But it would keep me away for a time from the killers and leg-breakers.

I got a big kiss from my lawyer and a real tight *abrazo* from my professor. Both our faces were really flushed when we separated. I knew I had someone I could really depend on, regardless. And he knew . . . what he knew.

Mom, I'll call as soon as I get to where I'm going.

TWENTY-SEVEN

Ralph remembers: *A summer evening in the year 1971, just weeks after graduating from Stuyvesant High School. His plans: to work into the next year at Uncle Felix's construction company, take night classes at Brooklyn College, save like mad while looking around for a college outside the city. A real campus, a small town. No more daily shuttling to and from Chambers Street, no more getting through Brooklyn on the lurching, squealing G train. Beautiful!*

They're coming out of the Meserole after seeing The Last Picture Show, *walking along Manhattan Avenue, the main drag of his Greenpoint, Brooklyn neighborhood: best friend and fellow Stuy graduate Paulie Breznick, Paulie's girlfriend Betty, Ralph and his date, Betty's cousin Rosemary. Betty and Rosemary are also recent grads, of Saint Joseph, the all-girls Catholic high downtown. Rosemary is as tall as Ralph, big features, clear blue eyes, blond upswept hair, rosy cheeks. A deep, heartfelt laugh. Lovely, tanned legs taking long, slightly awkward strides in her yellow summery dress. She plans to study acting. More than anything, she wants to be a stage actress. She loves Kim Stanley, Geraldine Page, Julie Harris. She's deeper, more serious than he had thought at first. Ralph really likes Rosemary, wants to date her again.*

She asks: "What about you? What are your plans? Are you going to be an engineer, like Paulie?"

"That's what I wanted when I got into Stuy. But not anymore. I want something closer to, well, how people live. The humanities. Maybe anthropology."

Rosemary gives him a wide, glistening smile. "That's great!"

"Hey," says Paulie, "my cousin Jerry's bar is just a couple of blocks down. Let's go there to celebrate. We all got proof of age, right?"

Paulie has had a card saying he was eighteen since his fifteenth birthday.

Ralph figures he'll nurse a beer.

They turn the corner at Nassau Street. Paulie and Betty are walking up ahead.

The bum comes out of the dark, then lurches forward, practically falling on Ralph. The bum stinks of wine, piss, vomit. Ralph backs up, pushes the bum off.

"You got a quarter, amigo? Hey, how 'bout two quarters?"

The bum's head moves back and forth as his blurry eyes try to focus in. His mouth works up, down and around. "Just two quarters, O.K. amigo?"

Then the bum pulls his head back and blinks. This time his mouth drops open in surprise. "Mi'jo! Como estás? How you, boy?"

Now Ralph pulls his head back and blinks. And blinks.

"Por favor, ayuda a tu papi. ¡Ayúdame!"

The bum's wriggling, scrawny fingers reach out to Ralph. He touches Ralph's arm. Ralph pulls away and hurries down the street. Rosemary runs to catch up to him.

Paulie, a few steps ahead, turns. "What's up?"

"Nothing," says Ralph.

"The poor guy," says Rosemary. "What was he saying in Spanish?"

"Nothing," says Ralph. "Nothing that means anything."

They have their drinks. Ralph takes Rosemary home by cab, to Williamsburg. He kisses her once, twice, before she ducks in the front door. He walks home. Just before he arrives at the apartment he shares with his mom and sister on Leonard Street, in front of the Polish National Catholic Church of the Resurrection, he throws up his guts.

Three months of construction work and night classes, occasional dates with Rosemary. Somehow, they don't really connect. Ralph wants a change in his life. He believes he soon will be drafted unless he enrolls in college. But something tells him that college is not the way to go. Something is eating at him. He knows.

For several days and nights, he walks the streets, looking for Juanito. What will he say, do, when he finds him?

He doesn't find Juanito. Maybe what Ralph saw that night was not his father, maybe it was an apparition. He never did see his father's hurt. It was a ghost.

Why should the guilt build in him? Wasn't his father the sonovabitch who deserted his family, who made no effort to stop drinking? Wasn't his father the guilty party? Of course!

On a bitter wintry morning, a cop in a patrol car finds the body of Juanito the bum on a pile of newspapers on the corner of Manhattan and Nassau, across the street from where Ralph had last seen and rebuffed his father.

The animal shit-musky algae smell as they slosh across the rice paddy to the edge of the jungle. Trees sparkling and crackling, like fireflies exploding in the branches. At first, it just stings at the top of the shoulder; then the burning begins, deep down, then widens until he passes out, comes back, out, in. The chopper picks him up and he bleeds on the floor and the medics patch him up.

Serves him right for enlisting.

A few weeks in hospital in Saigon, then he is sent home. Driving a Yellow Cab during the days, taking night classes at City College. Some months after, Ralph signs on for the Merchant Marines.

Ralph finishes reading The Odyssey, *of all places, in the port of Piraeus, where they are stuck for repairs. The monster storm they met out of Sicily bent the bow and damaged the propeller, the bilge pump, and the valves.*

Evening rush hour. A red sun melts in the gulf behind the port. Vehicles and pedestrians zig-zag all over the street, buses fuming, car and taxi horns honking; smoke, gas, and heat settle in the uncomfortable air. Ralph sits by himself at an outdoor café, sipping milky ouzo over ice, reading about the meetings of fathers and sons: Telemachus and Odysseus, Odysseus and Laertes.

"The heart of Odysseus was touched and his nostrils quivered as he looked up at his father, then he sprang toward him, flung his arms about him, and kissed him . . ."

It grips Ralph's heart. Just momentarily.

He still knew people at the SIU in Brooklyn and was able to make the arrangements for Richie, who was now a card-carrying member of the Seafarers International Union. Good luck *mi'jo*. My sort-of son.

Now he's finally ready. He'll set it in the 1920s. Max, an old salt, mentors a kid who goes to sea for the first time. Through their experiences in faraway lands, the surrogate son will bond with Max.

The young Ralph is the surrogate son. Richie also is the son. Max is Ralph's surrogate father. Wait, Max also is Ralph, who in his mind has adopted Richie. Ceylon, Singapore, Borneo of the colonial past stand for Puerto Rico of the colonial present . . .

Just write the damn thing!

TWENTY-EIGHT

Eva and I kept writing one another. I told her that I felt terrible about having to change our plans, to postpone our days and nights together. "But," I wrote, "we can, I hope, wait, because I believe our feelings toward one another are deep and true and will not fade with time."

When we had a mechanical problem and were stuck a week in Trinidad, I finally was able to finish *Love in the Time of Cholera*, the novel Eva sent me. While the rest of the crew was out celebrating carnival, I stayed in my bunk reading about the fifty-plus-year love affair between Florentino Ariza and Fermina Daza. I guess this says something about me, missing out on all the real-life fun for a by-the-book emotional experience. But I think, I hope, it says more about the power of the great García Márquez, whose fiction about never-ending love has fixed itself into my own reality.

If I could ever accomplish just a little of that!

Now, we're at sea again, on our way to deliver tropical fruit to England and Ireland. From there we go to . . . who knows? Supposedly, we don't get back to the Caribbean for another six months. I told Eva that we would definitely meet up then, that I would jump ship if I had to and bring her to Puerto Rico.

The work on a ship is mostly boring. Like the ordinary seamen before us, we still swab the decks, chip off rust, paint, and bring coffee and drinks to the officers. The crewmembers are more or less decent guys—give or take a couple of jerks. There have been a couple of fistfights, which I have stayed out of. Since I'm a college grad, I'm looked on by some as a kind of freak. But most of the others take me for what I am and we talk about everything, from baseball to movies to books.

Something weird happened during our stop to pick up mangoes and rum in Haiti. We docked in Port-au-Prince, and though I haven't been to Africa, yet, I'll bet the Haitian capital looks a lot like the poorest cities there. I was walking with Bobby Johnson, a shipmate, through an incredibly crowded street market that ran from the waterfront to the center of the city. It was near sunset, and the sky, the water and the skin of the people all were a burnished copper color. This bone-skinny kid, about 10 or 12, wearing a T-shirt with a picture of the Fugees and a Yankee cap with the lid over one ear, comes up and says in perfect Brooklynese, "Yo! Whaddup, dogs?"

Bobby Johnson, who's from Fort Greene, says, "Yo, li'l brother, whatcha doing here?" and the kid says, "I be born and I live all the time raised here, except for the one year, last year, I be living in New York when I ask a Bokor, you know, a Voodoo guy, to take me away from here, which he done for a year, even though every morning I wake up in my bed in my home here wit' my brothers and sisters. But I live in New York too and I see the big buildings and I go to the baseball and see the Yankees and I learn to talk American."

Bobby and I look at each other, wondering what this kid's hustle is. Will he ask for money to return to New York?

This is what he says next: "If you got the believing you could be anywhere. I think I will be in Paris next. I'm gonna go all over the worl'! See you guys." The kid faded into the crowd.

I've been writing a lot about the different ports we've been in, so far—Port-au-Prince, Port of Spain, Ponte-á-Pitre, Kingston, Oranjestad, Cartagena. I've been writing about the people on the different islands. I've been writing about our days and nights at sea, about my shipmates, about incidents on ship and on shore. I can't wait until we dock in Liverpool, then go on to Dublin, to Rotterdam, Bremerhaven, then, maybe, if I'm lucky, points south— Naples, Piraeus, Alexandria, Casablanca, through the Suez Canal, and on to other parts of the world.

So I'm looking forward to seeing different places, things. But there's still a heaviness in my heart. Will Eva and I ever get together again? How many times do you have to lose your love before some sort of happiness takes over for a reasonable time?

Still, I know this: You keep searching, you keep hoping, wondering, learning what it's all about.

You keep traveling, either across the seas or in your own head. Without the voyage, there's no settling down, no finding where you're really at.

ABOUT THE AUTHOR

Robert Friedman, who has had six novels published, was a reporter, columnist and city editor the *San Juan Star* in Puerto Rico for more than 20 years and was the newspaper's Washington correspondent until it folded in 2009. While in Puerto Rico, he was also special correspondent for the *New York Daily News*. In his fiction, he has explored the colorful and often struggling lives of island residents who try to cope, both personally and politically, with the highly ambivalent Puerto Rico-U.S. relationship. Born and bred in the Bronx, New York, he now lives in Silver Spring, Maryland, just outside of Washington, D.C.